Born Again

by

Alfred Lawson

Double 9
BOOKS

Born Again
by Alfred Lawson

Copyright © 2024

ISBN: 978-93-57273-83-1

Published by

DOUBLE 9 BOOKS

2/13-B, Ansari Road
Daryaganj, New Delhi – 110002
info@double9books.com
www.double9books.com
Tel. 011-40042856

This book is under public domain

Printed in India.

ABOUT THE AUTHOR

A professional baseball player, aviator, and utopian philosopher, Alfred William Lawson lived from March 24, 1869, until November 29, 1954. He played baseball from 1887 through 1916 as a player, manager, and league promoter before making a name for himself in the U.S. aircraft business. He released two early aircraft trade publications. He was given some of the early air mail contracts, but was eventually unable to carry them out. He is widely credited as the airliner's inventor. In order to produce military training aircraft, he established the Lawson Aircraft Company in Green Bay, Wisconsin. Later, he established the Lawson Airplane Company in South Milwaukee, Wisconsin, to construct commercial airplanes. His best opportunity for commercial aviation success was shattered when his ambitious Lawson L-4 "Midnight Liner" crashed on May 8, 1921, during the launch of a demonstration flight. In the 1920s, Lawson preached healthy lifestyle choices, such as vegetarianism, and asserted that he had discovered the key to a 200-year life span. He wrote many books about these ideas, many of which were written in his signature typography. Later, he promoted both the Lawsonian religion and his own philosophy, Lawsonomy.

CONTENTS

DEDICATION

One day, not many years ago, while walking along a street in Detroit, Michigan, I was stopped by a ragged and forlorn beggar, with the request for a few cents to buy something to eat.

I gave him a dime and walking on a few paces stopped to observe his following movements. Contrary to my supposition that perhaps he would enter a saloon and buy whiskey he went as fast as his weary legs would carry him in a straight course toward a restaurant on the opposite side of the street.

As he was about to enter the place his attention was attracted by a more pitiable wretch than himself standing outside who had but one leg, was partly blind, and whose nose was almost eaten off by disease.

He paused for a moment and looked sympathetically at the crippled beggar and then started again toward the door of the restaurant, but before entering he stopped once more to take another look, and after a few moments' hesitation he deliberately turned about, handed the other fellow the dime and walked away without feeding himself.

Of all the heroic deeds I have ever witnessed, I recollect none quite so grand and noble as this act, for notwithstanding this poor beggar may have been heir to every other weakness a human being could possibly contract, still he contained that spark of unselfish love for his fellow beings, without which no man is more than a mere brute, and for that reason I respectfully dedicate this work to his memory.

ALFRED WILLIAM LAWSON.

CHAPTER I

Judging from my own experience it is my opinion that many strange and wonderful events have happened during the past in which man took part, that have never been recorded.

Many reasons could be given for this, but the main causes perhaps, are that the participants have lacked the intelligence, education or literary ability to properly describe them.

In these respects I must admit my own inferiority. But I feel that should I not promulgate an account of my own remarkable life for the benefit of mankind then I would betray the trust nature has confided in me.

So I warn the exquisite literary critic and the over-polished individual who prefer fancy phrases to logical ideas, that this work may somewhat jar their delicate senses of perception.

And having offered these few remarks I shall introduce myself to the reader. My name is John Convert. The earth is my home and country. All men are my kin, be they white, black, red, yellow or brown. I was born somewhere on the Atlantic Ocean between Liverpool and New York while my parents were emigrating from England to America. My mother died giving me birth.

Whether or not it was because I first saw the light of day while in a state of transit that caused me afterwards to acquire a thirst for travel and adventure I cannot say, but true it is that during my whole life I have been constantly moving from place to place. Then again my father was a Methodist preacher and the good Lord ostensibly sent calls to him from every nook and corner of the United States, for as long as I can remember he too was continually changing abiding places. In fact, it seems to me now when I look back that he seldom preached twice from the same pulpit. Whether this was due to bad preaching or because he had the courage to tell the good church folk many plain truths concerning themselves, I know not, but I do know that in many ways my father was a very good man, and also a very learned man- -perhaps a little too learned to be wise, for, like most great scholars he may have forced so much book stuff into his brain that he left no room for progressive thoughts of his own. He was, however, quite unlike many clergymen of the present time who apparently think and certainly act as if their main work was to flatter and amuse the women.

My father was straightforward, honest, kind and truthful. He was dogmatic in his religious beliefs, combative by nature and never happier than when fighting the Devil in his own corner, as he expressed it. Furthermore, he was haughty, stubborn and egotistical, and these traits of character I inherited from him. But while I honestly inherited combativeness, stubbornness and egotism from my father, these characteristics became very objectionable to him when displayed by myself. So from my earliest childhood days there was a continual tug of war between us to see who would be master of the house.

There was one inheritance I received from my father, however, that I have always felt profoundly grateful to him for, namely, a sound physical constitution. One of his earnest teachings, which, by the way, was generally ridiculed, was that parents should not bring children into the world unless they themselves had led temperate lives and were in perfect health. In this respect he lived as he preached and practiced temperateness in all things.

As I grew up I was taught to take care of myself physically, as well as mentally and morally. At the age of eleven I was as large and strong as most boys of sixteen, and at sixteen there were few men who could outdo me in feats of strength and endurance. My education was limited to what I learned at the different public schools which I attended, and without exception I was always rated as the very worst boy of the whole institution. I do not believe that ever a day passed that I was not sent to the principal for refractory conduct, and in many instances I was suspended or expelled entirely. Fighting was my chief offence as I was always ready and anxious for a fistic encounter with any boy who was willing to battle. In short, I was a very unruly child with an independent spirit, who recognized the authority of nobody to give arbitrary commands. In consequence of these facts my father and I had frequent altercations and as my innate love for travel and adventure asserted itself I ran away from home when but eleven years old, an age when most children are mere babies, and started out in the world to paddle my own canoe.

I began to earn my own living by selling newspapers on the streets of Chicago, and from that time on became a wanderer upon the face of the earth; working at various occupations and engaging in many schemes and pursuits in an endeavor to pay my way through life, and during the next eleven years I not only visited every part of the United States, but nearly every country in the world, during which time I experienced enough adventures to fill many books if put into print, but as they have no bearing upon this narrative I must pass them by without mention. And so at the age of twenty-two, being then a worthless vagabond, I was aboard a three-masted schooner working my way from Australia to England as a common sailor. That was during the year of 1881.

CHAPTER II

Phrenologists after studying the bumps on my head have invariably told me that I lacked diplomacy. This, as I understand it, simply means an incapability of acting the hypocrite. And it does seem under the present system of human existence, that he who fails to practice hypocrisy finds innumerable obstacles to overcome, which otherwise might be avoided. So, lacking in this virtue, as diplomacy is sometimes styled, led me into trouble with nearly everybody with whom I had any dealings. Indeed, had it not been for this very defect in my nature, I should not have been forced to pass through the most remarkable life, I think, ever experienced by living man. And so the ship had barely passed out of the harbor before I had undiplomatically aroused the enmity of all the other seamen, and within two weeks I was thoroughly detested by every man aboard from the captain to the cook. The crew was composed of an unusually tough set of characters who avowed from the beginning that they did not like Yankees and would make life insufferable for me before reaching the next port. Fist fights became frequent and each one of the sailors took a "punch at my head" at different times, only to learn that I enjoyed that kind of sport and retaliated in a way that laid the offender up for repairs afterward. The fact that in these encounters I always gained an easy victory over my opponents caused a more intense feeling of bitterness to exist than ever, and to make matters worse the captain's wife, who was the only woman on the ship, took sides with me against all the others. This apparently angered the captain, for on one occasion, after he had given orders to have me put in irons for breaking one of my shipmate's ribs, and she interceded in my behalf, he became furious and threatened to have me thrown overboard. This threat, however, only had the effect of making me more stubborn and defiant. As a cowboy I had fought Indians and real bad men in the western states of America, hunted elephants in Africa, tigers in India, and roughed it as a gold seeker in Australia until I had become hardened against danger and absolutely fearless, so that a menace against my life did not worry me in the least. In fact, I really enjoyed the situation and dared the captain to do his worst.

We had been out of Sydney about four weeks, and although I did not know the exact latitude and longitude, I imagined we must have been a considerable distance to the south and east of Cape Colony. It seems to me now that I heard somebody say we were a little further south of the regular course taken by vessels sailing around the Cape. It was one of those pleasant nights in December, which one must experience in southern waters to appreciate, that I took my turn on watch in the forward part of the boat. It was past midnight and one of the darkest nights I have ever known. The sea was rather calm but a good breeze astern caused the ship to make good headway. I was all alone and paced back and forth from side to side peering out into space and darkness ahead. Occasionally, I would remain for several minutes leaning against one of the railings. Except for the splashing of the sea against the side of the ship, all was quiet. As I stood in one of my meditative moods, looking straight ahead, I was suddenly attracted by something which caused me to turn quickly and look in the opposite direction, and then I observed the forms of four men coming quickly toward me, but before I realized their object or had time to speak, they grabbed me by the arms and legs. I struggled furiously for several moments and freeing my hands, dealt one of them a vicious punch which felled him to the deck, and it seemed for awhile that I would shake them all off, when suddenly I received a terrible blow on the side of my head which partially stunned me, and during the instant of inactivity on my part I was raised bodily high in the air and plunged overboard into the waters below.

CHAPTER III

It was in a semi-conscious state that I struck the water head foremost, and it was by instinct, I suppose, that I immediately started to swim away from the side of the vessel.

Although I was a powerful swimmer it seemed as if I should never reach the surface again. The sudden and unexpected plunge had caused me to go into the sea with my mouth open and thereby swallow a large quantity of salt water. When almost on the verge of strangulation, however, by a supreme effort I finally managed to reach the air again, more dead than alive. It was then some time before I regained my breath and fully understood what had happened. I assure the reader that it was not a very pleasant sensation to find myself out in the middle of the ocean without even the support of a life preserver and the ship sailing away in the distance. During my adventurous career I had faced death a score of times without the slightest emotion or semblance of fright, but as I floated about on that broad expanse of water alone I then realized for the first time in my life what a tiny, helpless microbe I really was.

Oh, you little mortal known as man; you microscopical mixture of protoplasm and egotism; you atomical speck of ignorance and avarice; you who believe that the earth, moon, stars and all creation was manufactured for your special benefit; if you could only be shown your actual size in the universe as I was on that occasion, I think it would result in the eradication of some of your innate vanity and selfishness, thereby proving an incalculable blessing to you.

And now at last I was placed in a position whereby I could feel and reflect upon my own littleness. I had absolutely no hope of being saved from a watery grave, feeling that it was only a matter of an hour or two before I should succumb to the inevitable and sink to the bottom of the sea. Still I was unwilling to give up the few bones entrusted to my care until finally overcome by exhaustion and so I kept afloat by lying on my back and exerting myself as little as possible.

At length, however, my strength gave way entirely and I felt that the time had arrived when I must come face to face with the God whom I had been taught to believe in from infancy according to the Christian faith. Then it seemed that a million thoughts crowded themselves into my brain at the same time.

How would He receive me? What dire judgment would He pass upon me? Had I ever done anything to merit His pleasure? I could not recollect one good deed I had ever accomplished of sufficient importance to call to His attention, but on the contrary I recalled a thousand bad acts I should not have committed. I had spent a roving, aimless existence in which I had done practically nothing to increase the production or knowledge of the world, I had lived for myself alone--a life of mere pleasure seeking, without ever a thought of others' rights or happiness. I remembered that during a hunting expedition in Africa how I had once shot and killed seventeen spring-bok in one day, and how I had swelled up with conceit to know that I had destroyed the lives of that many living things. True, they were not human beings, but were they not creatures of nature as well as myself? What right had I to take the life of any living thing at all, let alone for mere pleasure? What excuse could I now offer if tried for that cowardly offence? Would I ask God's forgiveness? If so, would it be any better to ask Him to forgive me just before I died or immediately afterward? What difference would it make? Then again I wondered if God would have any more respect for me if after committing the deed I whined and begged for mercy. Would He not consider that cowardly on my part? Would He not think better of me if I went forward bravely and said: Here I am, O God, I know I have done wrong, now punish me as Thou see'st fit. What would I do if I were to occupy the Creator's position as supreme judge in a case of that kind? Would I not think far more of the man who would come forward courageously and take the punishment he deserved than the creeping, cringing and whining being who begged for mercy? Would God the Creator be more unreasonable about the matter than I, whom He had created?

I had always thanked God as well as my parents for the extraordinary physical strength and courage with which I was endowed, and during my life of trials and hardships that courage had never been shaken by man or beast, but now I felt that the crucial test was about to be applied. Would the courage the Almighty gave me weaken when about to face Him who had bestowed it upon me?

With these and similar thoughts passing through my mind and my strength exhausted, I took one long breath and sank beneath the water.

CHAPTER IV

Sinking slowly down with a feeling of drowsiness stealing away my senses, I was suddenly awakened by my body coming to an abrupt stop and resting upon some hard substance. My first impression was that I had collided with some huge sea-monster and was about to be devoured. So placing my hands and feet firmly upon it I sprang upward with all the force I could command in an effort to get out of its reach, but to my great surprise my head and half of my body shot out of the water into the air above and down I came again square upon my feet with a jolt that caused my teeth to rattle. And there I stood with my head and shoulders out of the water while my lungs inhaled long draughts of pure fresh air. I was too astonished to think and too weak to move, so I just stood there motionless until I had regained my equilibrium. I could never forget how sweet life seemed to me at that time. For a long time I remained standing there without giving a thought as to what I was resting upon, and when I did direct my attention to the question I was incapable of forming a satisfactory solution to the mystery. According to the charts there was no land in that part of the ocean. Could it be a whale, I wondered? The more I thought of it the more perplexed I became. The night was very dark and I could see nothing about me in any direction, so I concluded that the only thing to do was to remain standing just where I was until daybreak. It was a long and tedious wait and I suffered much from stiffness and cold, but at last dawn appeared and I anxiously strained my eyes, looking about in every direction. Then my head nearly burst with a feeling of joyousness, for within two hundred yards of me I discerned the outline of what appeared to be a hill of rocks protruding from the deep, and as the light grew brighter I started to wade slowly towards it. This was an extremely tiresome undertaking, as the bed upon which I had been resting was very rocky and uneven and I received many bruises before finally reaching its base. My limbs too were thoroughly numb and almost refused to work, but with each step ahead the water became shallower and my progress less arduous. As I went forward I thought it was by the miraculous hand of God that my life had been saved, for the time being at least. Then, again, it occurred to me, that if it was the hand of the Almighty that saved me, it must have been by His hand also that I was thrown overboard, for if He directed the one act He must have surely directed the other. So why blame the sailors for attempting to take my life if it was God's will that it should be done?

Reaching the base of the rocks in a feeble condition and staggering like a man under the influence of liquor, I threw myself down and went to sleep just as the sun peeped over the horizon.

Several hours later I awakened with a start to find the burning sun directly overhead and my body dripping with perspiration, my throat parched and an awful feeling of thirst within me. My tongue felt as though it was several inches thick and it seemed as though I would choke immediately for the want of something to drink. Aside from the thirst, however, I felt considerably refreshed and sprang to my feet with my usual agility.

The first thing that attracted my attention as I looked about in a curious manner, was that this strange pile of stone which protruded from the sea, bore evidence of having once been a part of some mammoth building which had apparently been shaken down and now lay in a chaotic heap. Some of the stones were of tremendous size and different in shape and quality from any others I have ever seen. Their designs showed that wonderful skill must have been employed by the workmen who originally cut and fit them into position. The whole mass formed a sort of a ragged hill about one hundred feet in diameter and the highest point about forty feet above the sea level.

In looking about, I discovered to my great delight that among the crevices of the rocks there were many little places which acted as basins to store up water from the recent rains, and I immediately took advantage of these conditions to quench my thirst and bathe my face and head. This done I began climbing up toward the top of the pile. It took considerable time and patience to make the ascent, as the stones were massed together in a most irregular and precipitous manner. Reaching the highest point, I eagerly scanned the surrounding horizons with the hope of seeing some passing ship, but nothing except sky and water met my gaze.

Seating myself upon the topmost rock, I became buried in the depths of meditation, and as I sat perched up there alone without even a glimpse of a sea-fowl for companionship I felt as if I was the only living thing extant; in fact, I actually imagined myself as being the center and objective point of the universe. God in His great wisdom had flung me there for some purpose or other and was watching my movements to the exclusion of everything else, so I thought. Aye, even the warmth from the rays of the sun had been arranged for my special benefit. How big a little faith will make one feel sometimes.

For several hours I remained in one position, musing over my strange situation and wondering what the final outcome would be. At last, after the sun had gone down and darkness began to encircle me, I decided to look about and find a suitable place to lie down and sleep for the night. So I began to climb from rock to rock until I had reached the opposite side of the jagged plateau, when suddenly one of the great stones wobbled, I lost my balance and slid down an incline into a sort of a pit. Then my feet struck something which momentarily stopped my unexpected descent, but it proved to be a mere shell, and crashing through it I landed with a violent jolt about ten feet further below. Although somewhat stunned and a trifle confused by the suddenness of the fall, I quickly regained my equanimity and looking upward I saw a small hole which my body had passed through, the shaggy rocks above, the dark sky and a few stars, but the strangest thing of all was, that the grotto into which I had fallen was as light as day.

CHAPTER V

After all I had passed through during the preceding twenty-four hours, then to be suddenly cast from the outer darkness into a hole as light as if illuminated by the mid-day sun was a revelation that caused me to seriously doubt my own senses. But having spent a life of travel and adventure in which I had faced many unexpected dangers and inexplicable sights, I soon regained my normal presence of mind and began to look around with considerable interest. I was now fully convinced that the great pile of stone which I had so strangely reached had at one time formed a gigantic structure moulded together by human ingenuity.

The enclosure I found myself within might have been a hallway of the edifice, but it was hard to positively distinguish it as such, for the building in falling had placed things in an almost unrecognizable condition. Some of the great stones from above had passed through the ceiling and floor, while others had become wedged together before reaching the surface, thus forming a very ragged and peculiar aperture.

In places where there were no obstructions I noticed a beautiful white marble floor, while here and there a fragment of the walls showed that the art of decorating had at one time reached a degree of proficiency quite unapproachable by our modern artists. The space I found myself in was too irregular in its outlines to form an adequate idea of what it might have been used for. In some places I had to stoop to pass along, while in others I was forced to climb over great blocks of stone.

After being in this passage about half an hour making an inspection of the premises, I discovered a small opening which led into another apartment. It appeared that a great door had separated the two rooms, but had apparently become broken with the fall of the building and left a space barely wide enough for my body to pass through. So in I went. Or out I went, I was not quite sure which, for after squeezing through the doorway a scene presented itself to my astonished gaze that I must confess my inability to properly describe.

The view before me was a mammoth park with its variety of trees, flowers and shrubbery of every possible description.

Straight ahead in the distance and plainly discernible was a running brook which flowed along in a devious course and emptied into a lake far beyond. And there, in all its majesty was the sun just sinking behind the horizon, its brilliant radiance forming the most beautiful effects of colorization upon the distant clouds it has ever been my good fortune to behold.

I stood in motionless reverence for several minutes as my mind expanded with wonder at the magnificent panorama, while my nostrils inhaled a most delicious fragrance from the innumerable plants which seemed to put new life into my enervated body.

What strange phenomena is this, I soliloquized? On the outside of the earth the sun had gone down and darkness prevailed, while down here, in under its crust I found it blazing away in all its splendor. In fact it seemed that an entirely new world had suddenly been thrown in front of me. Was I really alive or had I passed into some other world, was the next question to enter my mind. I remembered that I had fallen a considerable distance into this strange place and was somewhat stunned in the tumble. Perhaps, thought I, my body is still lying somewhere among the rocks above while this is only my spirit wandering about in a fanciful manner. But no, looking downward I plainly saw my massive frame dressed in sailor's clothes just as I had left the ship and I was positive of being alive, awake, and in my right senses. And the wonders multiplied. Looking to the right of the entrance, a short distance away, I observed a marble platform elevated about two feet from the ground, in the midst of huge flower-beds and shaded by large trees, upon which sat a number of men, silent and motionless, with various musical instruments in their hands as if they had just finished playing and were taking a short rest. These instruments were of an entirely different pattern from any I had ever seen. And the men! Oh, if I only had the power to show them to my fellow beings as I saw them. What an imposing, noble looking lot they were. They were all about the same size and not one of them could have been less than eight feet in height. In looking at them closely, I noticed that they possessed most magnificent physiques. They were neither fat nor lean and their well-groomed bodies showed plainly that no horse or piece of machinery ever received better care or attention. While they appeared to be from thirty to forty years in ages, not one of them wore a mustache, beard or any other shaggy decoration of the face. Their foreheads were broad and massive and extended to the center of their splendidly shaped craniums. Extraordinary intelligence, kindness and gentleness showed forth from every feature of their handsome countenances. Judging from their well-proportioned frames, each one looked powerful enough to battle single handed with an elephant. Judging from their faces not one of them would have hurt a flea. Each man appeared to be buried in the depth of thought--serious thought-- notwithstanding every physiognomy plainly showed that the utmost happiness and contentment existed within each, and good will between all of them. The skin of their faces, hands and feet was as white as snow, transparent, and backed by a beautiful pink. At first sight I thought they were the gods. Uniformly clothed in closely fitting garments from the ankles to the neck, their superb forms showed complete symmetrical perfection. The hue of their raiment was indescribable for I had never seen the like before. In fact the colors actually appeared to change before my steady gaze. Their feet were bare, very shapely, and the toes of greater length than ordinarily.

As I stood rooted to the ground and viewed them with intense admiration, I wondered why they did not speak or take notice of my presence. But finally in order to attract their attention I shouted, hello. My voice sounded rather harsh and peculiar on this occasion, and was more like the bray of an ass than anything else, but they made no motion as if they heard me, or were aware of my existence. Walking over to the nearest one, I reached up and touched him on the shoulder. Then I sprang back in amazement, for instead of giving any sign of recognition he merely placed his instrument in position, as did all the others, and with slow, graceful movements began to play. The first strains of music, although distinct and supernaturally grand, seemed to be miles away but gradually increased in sound as if coming nearer and nearer. At the same time I observed that the musicians, who were not only using both hands in the manipulation of their instruments but with graceful dexterity their feet as well, were becoming enthusiastic and appeared to throw their very lives and souls into the work. If at first while inactive they appeared to be extraordinarily intellectual beings, now in action they looked divine. Their eyes blazed like miniature suns shooting forth sparks of a thousand different hues. It seemed as if the very music itself came from the expression of their faces. And on, on, on, came the intoxicating strains, increasing in volume and excellence until I imagined that all heaven had broken loose in one great effort to charm my feeble senses, and then with a thunderous climax it ceased instantly, the musicians smiled and bowed pleasantly to one another, and then resumed their former attitudes.

No mortal's pen could describe my ecstasy while listening to the music produced by this body of--I must say heavenly creatures. There was something strange and analogous about it, too, that seemed to recall a mysterious dream or vision I had once passed through. Whether it was caused by the music or the kindly expressions of love for one another on the faces of the players I know not, but nevertheless great tears spontaneously rolled down my cheeks, the first I ever recollect having shed, and at the conclusion of the piece I remained transfixed to the spot for several minutes in deep cogitation.

Once more, however, my inquiring nature aroused me and I walked over toward the leader. His face was turned slightly in another direction, so I decided to step up on the platform, get squarely in front of him and look straight into his eyes. So with a light movement I sprang for the rostrum. But instead of reaching it my foot and head struck--not the platform but solid wall, and a second later I found myself in a heap on the ground. Then I started to think. Next I began to feel and finally a broad grin overspread my face, for the scene before me was not real after all, but a wonderful painting on the interior of the building.

CHAPTER VI

Putting my hand against the surface and walking along I discovered that this great scene which appeared to stretch away into the distance for several miles, including the trees, brook, lake, sun, clouds, sky, and everything else, was painted on the wall, ceiling and floor, of a circular room. The ceiling was arranged in the shape of a dome, while the floor made a concave connection with the wall. The whole apartment could not have been over fifty feet in diameter. The entire room was covered by one painting, and so well had the work been done that the only way I could discern the difference between the real and artistic scene was by extending my hands in front of me and feeling my way along.

But what about the music? Surely I heard it, and without doubt the skilled musicians had performed their work right before my eyes. And the sun, the light, and the fragrance from the flowers, what about these? While in a state of perplexity at not being able to understand these mysterious things, my eyes fell upon something which I had not noticed previously, at the same time causing me to give a sudden start as if pierced by an electric shock.

To the left of the door through which I had entered and lying in a reclining position upon a bed of flowers, similar in shape to a modern sofa, was the most beautiful object, I think, ever created--a woman. And such a woman. Oh, ignorant humanity, why do you not breed all women like that one? Although nearly twenty-three years have passed since then, still the vision of her is as fresh upon my mind now as at that moment when my eyes first beheld her. And as I think of her now I am unable to repress the tears from filling my eyes, strong man that I am.

Dressed in a tight-fitting costume like those worn by the men, with the addition of a net-like drapery of light material entwined about her, and lying in a comfortable position partly on one side, with her lovely head resting upon one arm, her shapely body and limbs posed gracefully and her eyes closed in slumber, she impressed me as being the queen of the universe.

This is the most beautiful part of the whole picture, thought I, taking a few steps forward. What artist's imagination could ever have created such a sublime and realistic work? As I stood in reverent contemplation of her my admiration was unbounded. It seemed as if my feelings would burst within me. My first love for woman was then and there confirmed for all time. I decided I would stay and spend the rest of my days right there, silently attesting my everlasting devotion to that divine likeness of ideality. Had I not discovered that the whole thing was a work of art, I should have felt positive that she was really alive and merely lay there in peaceful repose. Then a sudden thought passed through my mind which gradually expanded into an irresistible desire; I would press my lips to hers and thereby seal my love forevermore.

Trembling like a timid school-boy I advanced closer. How lovely she appeared. How real. Bending forward and putting my head in juxtaposition to hers it seemed as if I actually heard her heart beat. It may have been my own. With my face flushed and feeling that perhaps I might be taking an unfair advantage of one who would not appreciate my caress, I tenderly touched her lips with mine. For another moment of such indescribable ecstasy I would gladly pass through all the imaginary tortures of the infernal regions. But it ended there.

No sooner had our lips come together than I became aware of the fact that the adorable object before me was real and not artificial as supposed. As if by magic her mouth twitched slightly and her whole frame quivered perceptibly; then she opened her eyes and finally with a most graceful spring she landed squarely upon her feet directly in front of me. I jumped backward in utter amazement. And there we stood face to face staring into each other's eyes. I then noticed that she was about seven feet in height and although not lean still there was not an ounce of superfluous flesh on her serpent-like figure. Like the men, she too was bare footed, and her hair, a dark silky texture, was short and very artistically arranged. Her snow white face, transparent with pink, was the acme of loveliness, with an expression of gentleness, purity and modesty plainly stamped upon every feature. Her dazzling eyes sparkled with the brilliancy of huge diamonds. Evidently she was as much astonished as myself at the strange course of events. Although she did not speak still I received an impression from her as if put into so many words which plainly said: "John, am I dreaming or what awful experiment have you attempted to transform yourself into such a hideous creature?" I tried to speak but my first effort nearly choked me. Then in a voice which seemed to be unusually coarse I finally blurted out: "My dear lady, will you kindly tell me who or what you are?" These words seemed to puzzle her more than ever and after hurriedly glancing about the room she looked me over carefully from head to foot. Speaking once more I said, "Madame, can you understand my language?" Then I received another strange but unmistakable impression which replied: "I can understand your thoughts but not your babble." "Are you able," she continued telepathically, "to give an explanation of this extraordinary metamorphosis?" "The only information I can offer," answered I, "will be cheerfully given. My name is John Convert, late seaman aboard the schooner Brawl, bound from Sydney to London. Last night I was thrown overboard by my shipmates and after floating about the deep for several hours I landed upon this pile of ruins surrounded by the sea. In making an investigation of the exterior I lost my foothold, fell into a crevice and breaking through a thin crust I landed in the outer passageway which finally led me into this room. I must confess that everything here is as inexplicable to me as I appear to you." As I spoke she seemed to be laboring under intense mental excitement and tears came to her eyes.

"I understand it all now," she made known to me in her mysterious way, "the experiment failed."

"What experiment was that?" questioned I in surprise.

Looking me straight in the eye as though trying to impress upon my mind the importance of her communication, she answered, "the attempt of man to change the course of the earth in space."

CHAPTER VII

"And so you inform me that there is nothing left of beautiful Sageland but a heap of ruins surrounded by the sea," mused the lovely--the idea struck me to name her Arletta--"tell me what happened to the rest of my people."

"Not knowing anything about the matter it is impossible for me to answer that question," replied I; "and although I have traveled through nearly every country on earth still no such people as you or the magnificent objects represented in that picture have ever come to my attention before. In fact I have never read of such a race or even heard of a country by the name of Sageland."

At this remark she turned abruptly and walked--or rather flew, so easy and graceful were her movements--over to a portion of the wall and looked long and earnestly into a peculiar instrument, then returning she said: (without the use of words) "according to my chronometer, more than four thousand two hundred and thirty years have elapsed since the awful catastrophe."

"Four thousand, two hundred and thirty years!" ejaculated I, "great heavens, that must have been about the time of the flood." "What flood?" inquired she.

Then I proceeded to tell her how in those days the people of the world being so wicked that God during a terrible fit of anger made it rain for forty days and forty nights, causing the destruction of every living thing on earth except one Noah, his family and a male and female of every animal, bird and insect, who were saved by being taken aboard of a huge ark built for the purpose by Noah. And then after every living thing not aboard the boat was destroyed, how the waves receded, Noah and his flock were safely landed upon a mountain peak, and God put a bow into the sky as a pledge that he would never do such a thing again. Arletta appeared somewhat amused at my recital of the story and at its conclusion merely remarked: "Noah evidently had more good sense than his god." Then she added: "As to the rainbow, that was seen by the inhabitants of the earth millions of years before Noah's time."

"So the world has retrogressed during the past four thousand years," mused she sadly.

"Retrogressed! No indeed, the world has made great progress and has now reached a wonderful state of civilization," answered I, proudly.

Motioning me to an opposite position she majestically seated herself upon the couch and after seriously looking at me for some time she finally said: "This is one of nature's most extraordinary proceedings and there are many things I wish to talk with you about, but before going into the details of this matter I am anxious to get a view of the world as it exists now. You have observed that unlike the lower animals, in which rank unfortunately you belong at the present time"--here I interrupted her by bursting forth into loud laughter, not because I enjoyed being called an animal myself but at the thought of how some of my civilized friends would feel if informed that they were lower animals. My intervention, however, not disturbing her in the least, she resumed: "In our nomenclature your species was known as the Apeman, and represented in the chain of evolution the link between the Ape and Man. Our scientists placed the Apeman within the ranks of the lower animals for reasons I shall make clear later. But to continue, you have observed that unlike yourself I have been conversing with you without the use of the voice but with the mind, the most effectual agent of communication and one of the senses the Apeman has not cultivated. Now I shall show you how to see without eyes.

"Mind sight is an occult force which was exercised to great advantage by my people. This force eliminates both distance and obstruction and exposes to view the object sought even if it is located on the opposite side of the globe. Any mind, if sufficiently strong, can contract distance and bring any mundane scene within its range while penetrating solid matter as if it did not exist at all. So by utilizing this power, which I possess to a considerable degree, it is my intention to make a hurried survey of the earth's surface in order to obtain an exact idea of present conditions. Furthermore, by the subtle concentration of our mind forces together I shall convey to your inner vision the actual scenes witnessed by myself, and you shall act as my mental consort on a trip around the world."

After the many wonderful things I had already seen it was my opinion that there was nothing impossible for this beautiful woman to perform, so I mildly informed her that I was at her service, and ready for the journey to begin.

"Well then," said she, "before starting I wish to warn you that no matter what you see, hear or feel on this trip you must not disturb our observation with your primitive babble, apish laughter or by trying to offer any comments whatsoever."

At this remark I was brought to a realization of the fact that Arletta, whom I so ardently loved, aye even worshipped, was treating me in about the same manner as I would have treated a pet monkey had I been teaching it some new tricks. She evidently regarded my smiles and feelings for her with about the same consideration as I should have given to those of some grinning female baboon had it been trying to make love to me. Her last thoughts, therefore, aroused my sensitive nature, and a violent outburst of temper was the result. I did not mind being called an Apeman so much, but hated the idea of being treated like one, so working myself into a passion I severely censured her, and with much bluster and many gestures endeavored to impress upon her mind how much superior I was to what she had imagined. It was some time before my anger abated, and then I noticed that she appeared quite unmoved by my wrath but sat looking calmly and alternately at me and one of the figures in the picture, while her face bore an expression of sadness and pity. Then I felt ashamed to think of what a lack of self-control I had exhibited, and humbly begged her pardon.

"But now," said Arletta, and I fancied that she called me John, "your soul is at present running the machinery of a very inferior mind and body which plainly shows all the cruel passions and idiotic ideas of the Apeman. This has happened through no fault of your own but is the result of circumstances over which you had no control so that you are not responsible for your present condition. I now say however that you have been chosen by nature for a great and glorious work and from this time forward you must make use of your reasoning faculties for reasonable purposes and cast aside all the animal passions, silly ideas and antiquated superstitions which you have inherited from the ignorant of ages, and begin afresh. Before starting on our journey perhaps it would be well for us to take some refreshments in order that our minds may remain strong and clear during the trip. We take our nourishment in a different way from you cannibals," said Arletta, as she went to one of the artificial flower gardens, began inhaling and motioned me to do likewise. "But we are not cannibals," I mildly remonstrated, "we do not kill and eat human beings." "Do you not kill and eat the flesh of other living things?" inquired she. "Yes," replied I, "our diet consists of the flesh of birds, fish and cattle which God with great wisdom created for that purpose." "Did he? Then you must worship a cannibal god, for it is but a very short step between eating the flesh of your own species and that of others. That is one reason why our scientists ranked the Apeman with the lower animals. But come, inhale this perfume and see if it is not far more refreshing and less disgusting than to fill your stomach with roasted flesh."

At her suggestion I stationed myself near the flower bed which contained a large variety of the most beautiful plants I had ever seen. She touched several of them lightly and immediately the air was saturated with a most delicious fragrance caused, no doubt, by an automatic arrangement concealed within each flower. I stood like one in a most delightful dream inhaling the invigorating fumes, and with each succeeding breath my body became stronger and my mind brighter until I thought I should surely die from the effects of exuberant joy, when my attention was attracted by Arletta, who said: "Come, you greedy little pig, don't you know when you have had enough?" Then she added, "but I forgot that among your species greediness is considered a virtue."

CHAPTER VIII

"Greediness considered a virtue among my species." Surely I must have misunderstood her, thought I, once more seating myself, preparatory to beginning my mental journey with Arletta. And I was glad to know that she would shortly view our civilization as it existed, feeling positive that she would then change her ideas regarding my species being lower animals. I felt that it was my own fault because she harbored such an opinion and that I was to blame for being such a poor representative of my race for her to judge by.

"Now, let's be off," said she, "as I feel that my time will be short with you and we had better make the best of it while it lasts." "Time short with you." Those words gave me more pain than if a sword had been thrust through my body. "By all the gods of eternity, I would not care to live ten minutes if anything happened to that heavenly being," thought I, gazing at her with rapturous feelings of tenderness. "Call me a lower animal, a hideous creature or a greedy pig, and treat me like one if you will, but do not leave me. Stay and let me be your slave forever." Those were my sincere thoughts. She understood them, but made no response.

Settling back in a comfortable position with my eyes fastened upon Arletta in loving adoration, the scene changed instantly and I found myself once more upon the rocks in the middle of the sea. The sun was just rising in the east and another day was begun. Then our meteoric flight commenced, and quicker than it takes to relate I was high up among the clouds and peering down at a familiar landscape. I recognized the location at once as the district occupied by and surrounding Cape Town, South Africa.

I had been there before. But how peculiar everything appeared now as I looked down from above. I could plainly discern the harbor and great tableland in the scene before me, although apparently shrunk in size, but the city itself resembled a little toy village, while the largest ships in the harbor reminded me of the tiny boats I used to construct when a child and float about in the bath-tub. But where, oh where, was the greatest of all exalted things--that for which the entire universe and all that it contains therein was constructed--mighty man? He could not be seen. In fact he was as completely invisible as the pestilential germ on the back of a sick flea. "If I only had a microscope," thought I, "perhaps I could see him." Then I began to descend, until finally I discovered innumerable little creepers moving about in all directions. They were men. At first sight they looked to be about the size of ants, but as I got closer to the earth they increased in bulk until they appeared to be at least three inches in height, and then their importance became noticeable. As they moved about in great numbers and I came into close proximity with them, I observed that the actions of some was apparently sensible but that the doings of the most of them was positively ridiculous. For instance, here was one set of creatures diligently toiling to produce something and getting nothing, while here was a set of idlers doing absolutely nothing but receiving everything. The real producer of all the necessities and luxuries of life was actually giving nine-tenths of the fruits of his labor to a class of loafers and schemers who took it as a divine right, and then begrudged him the one-tenth he received of his own production. I observed that for every one of these producers there were ten non-producers who spent their time and efforts devising the best ways and means to confiscate that which had been produced. It seemed strange that the producer would allow this state of affairs to exist; but he did, and seemed quite elated sometimes to think that the non-producer would permit him to live at all. I noticed that most of the non-producers were fat and bloated from being over-fed and from guzzling prepared liquors, and that they were clothed with the finest materials the producer could contribute, while the producers themselves were lean and hungry looking objects, and were dressed in rags. I had seen these same things many times before without giving them any consideration, but now for the first time, I felt that there was something wrong with the people of the world. It seemed to me now that the entire system of human endeavor had been started wrong and was running along upside down. But what was the cause of this curious state of affairs? One word alone explained it all-- Selfishness. And then there came to me a sentence, the imprint of which has never been effaced from my memory, viz: "Selfishness is the root of all evil; eradicate selfishness from all human beings and the earth win be heaven."

Oh, dear reader, go over those few words again, and again; ten times; fifty times; one hundred times if necessary to thoroughly impress their full meaning upon your intellect. Study them; practice them; teach them; sing them to all the world. Take them for your everlasting motto and you will have no need for all the stupid theories ever created by man. "Eradicate selfishness from all human beings and the earth will be heaven."

And now I observed that great numbers of these little men were being unloaded from the various ships in the harbor, and upon landing started immediately in a northerly direction. I understood the reason. Gold had been discovered in the Transvaal, and thousands upon thousands were coming from every quarter of the globe in anticipation of getting some of this metal. And what is there about gold that caused people to go such vast distances and bear many hardships and even risk their lives in desperate efforts to obtain it? Is there more real value to gold than other metals? Not at all. There is no more intrinsic value to gold than brass, but centuries ago, a semi-savage glutton discovered that he could not eat all the swine he could raise nor legally steal all his contemporaries could breed, so he originated a plan whereby he could secure for himself what others had produced through the agency of a financial system in which gold could be used as a medium of exchange. He found that he could get other and less crafty savages to go and dig the gold for him in return for swine. He also found that the breeders would exchange swine for gold. So he started by giving the diggers one swine for ten ounces of gold and the breeders one ounce of gold for ten swine. This transaction he called business. This system of business has been handed down from generation to generation until it has become a part of man's very nature. He knows very little of anything else. Gold being the financial medium of business he is taught to crave it in his infancy and as he grows older gold becomes his idol--his God. In order to gain possession of gold or its equivalent man forgets his soul and sells his honor. He is willing to crush the weak, cheat, steal or even murder his fellow beings to obtain it. And no matter whether he has little or much of it he considers any person insane who dare suggest the abolition of the financial system which permits individual accumulation and breeds selfishness and crime.

With a change of mind, I landed thousands of miles further north into the interior of uncivilized Africa, the home of wild beasts. Here something occurred which caused me to think that after all, perhaps Arletta was right in classing my species with the lower animals. Under ordinary conditions I should not have given the incident a second thought, but now my mind being directly connected with hers, I was, no doubt, impressed in the same manner as she while viewing these things.

A party of English gentlemen were on a hunting expedition. They appeared to be intelligent beings of aristocratic birth. Men whom the average individual would take as examples to emulate. But here they were in Africa, thousands of miles from home, with the sole purpose of killing something for pleasure. A short distance away was a family of lions; a male, female and several cubs. The lion and lioness lay close together, apparently casting loving glances at one another and enjoying the antics of the little ones who were playing together nearby. Occasionally the little ones would run over and kiss their elders in a most affectionate way, which seemed to greatly please the parents. Never have I seen a family of human beings display so much real affection toward each others as this family of lions. But alas, their happiness was at an end. Man's appetite for killing must be appeased. One of the hunters had caught sight of the happy little family, and slinking behind a tree before his presence became known to the lions he signaled to his comrades, who sneaked forward from tree to tree until they were within easy range of their prey. Then fixing their rifles and taking deliberate aim at the unsuspecting victims, and without giving them any chance to defend themselves or little ones, these so-called brave and civilized hunters pulled the triggers and the happy old lion and the lioness simultaneously expired, pierced by a dozen bullets. And what became of the little ones? The sight was too pitiable to describe. After the effects of the first fright, caused by the noise of the shots, had passed, they instinctively rushed to their parents for protection. Oh, the anguish depicted upon the faces of these little things when they discovered that their loving progenitors were no more. Their looks and moans were heartrending. But there were others made happy. A sudden shout of joyousness burst forth from the throats of a dozen civilized men who eagerly rushed from behind their fortresses to view the work of destruction. They had displayed fine marksmanship and were greatly pleased. Good shooting, said one of the brave fellows. Splendid, exclaimed another. But what shall we do with the cubs? asked the third. Better finish them also, remarked a fourth, as I am very fond of cub meat, and would like nothing better than a broiled steak from one of their little carcasses. After a few minutes' parley a decision was reached that it would be uncivilized to allow the little ones to wander about the jungle alone for fear that they might become the prey for other wild animals, so they killed them also; and filled their stomachs with them. And after they were through, a flock of vultures descended and finished the work. Men and vultures are somewhat alike in this respect; they both eat the flesh of carcasses. But a good word can be said for the vultures, however; they never kill.

CHAPTER IX

I t on the globe through the power of mind sight, and I was enabled to see any terrestrial occurrence as well as if having been on the spot in person. In fact, being under the direct is not my intention to give a full descriptive account of my peculiar journey around the world with Arletta, nor to recount the many strange things witnessed. Suffice it to mention that we visited nearly every country influence of Arletta's perception, conditions appeared much more comprehensive to me than ever before and I felt like some great judge looking down upon the earth and its inhabitants with an impartial eye. And somehow these inhabitants did not seem to impress me as being in such a high state of intelligence as I had formerly been led to believe they were. Everywhere human beings were fighting and snarling amongst themselves like ferocious beasts. Their universal law granted the right of the strong to victimize the weak either through the power of physical or mental force. In fact it was considered a divine right for men of superior intellects to receive more of the fruits of the earth than those of smaller mental capacity. One-half of the world was over-fed while the other half was under-fed. Aside from a slight difference in political and religious theories, the characteristics of all the peoples of the world were the same; the predominant features being greed, vanity, egotism, intemperance, gluttony, fraud, theft, bribery, deceit, brutality, murder, superstition and filth. Even America, the much boasted land of the free, the country which God in his infinite wisdom had taken from the bad English and given to the good Americans, contained people with these traits, and the so-called great men of this country appeared like a lot of silly little pigmies engaged in an eternal quarrel over a few trinkets. Few of them could see further than their own noses unless it was to see something that would increase their own selfish desires. Equality, of which these people boasted so much, existed merely in their imaginations. The actual meaning of equality, as the Americans understood it, was that the physical and mental gladiators and weaklings alike were put into one great prize ring and given an opportunity to fight for their lives and nature's gifts. Those who were capable of battering down and trampling upon their adversaries were legally entitled to all the luxuries the earth provided and more than they could use, but those who were unfortunate enough to have been born weaklings and were unfit to cope successfully with the huge monsters in the ring, were crushed in the struggle.

Fraud was the slogan of the government officials and nearly all of them practiced it, from the highest to the lowest functionary. Money was the power behind the curtain and he who had the largest bank account was catered to like an over-grown hog surrounded by a lot of suckling pigs. "God helps those who help themselves" was their accepted motto. In other words, God helps the strong and not the weak. If the Creator gives any of His attention to the innumerable bickerings of these earthly microbes He must feel greatly flattered by having this splendid motto thrust upon Him, for according to it, one was supposed to go to the assistance of the man who could swim, while he who could not, must be left to drown.

A certain so-called great American, one Mr. Moundbuilder by name, expressed great faith in this doctrine. By employing thousands of his fellow men to do the hard work while he sat in an easy chair and confiscated the difference between what they earned and what he paid them, he accumulated several hundred million dollars for his own use. About the time he was ready to die he learned to his great sorrow that it was necessary to leave all this wealth behind. So he decided to bequeath it to only those who were sufficiently strong and willing to continue his policy of crushing the weak and incidentally erect some monuments to his own memory. After much consideration as to how the strong would derive the most benefit from his ill-gotten goods, he concluded that the weak-minded and sickly creatures who were bred from the system he abetted and the over-worked and under-fed laborer would have no opportunity to read books, so he established hundreds of Moundbuilder libraries and Moundbuilder universities in all parts of the world. To those who were already strong enough to reach a position where they could enter a university and did not really need his aid, the idea was a grand one, as it would help to increase their strength, thereby making it much easier for them to confiscate what the weaklings could produce in the future. Thus the plan to make the strong stronger, the weak weaker, and Moundbuilder immortal, would be perpetuated. But the cherished hopes of Mr. Moundbuilder in this respect will never be realized, for the day is not far distant when earthly mortals will be able to reason and then he will be recognized simply as a vain-glorious old humbug.

Another celebrated American who was classed among the great men of the day was a certain Mr. Porkpacker. This individual conducted an establishment where thousands of animals, bred for the purpose, were slaughtered daily. He had accumulated millions of blood-stained dollars in this way, and was generally conceded to be a man of great business ability. He was pointed out to the rising generation as one of the most successful men in the country whose example should be followed. Just pause a moment and think of it. Here was a man who directed a business where thousands of living things were murdered daily, set forth as a good example to follow just because he had secured millions of dollars by the operation. Oh, ye mortals! Man considers the wolf a blood-thirsty beast because he kills and eats the flesh of human beings for subsistence. What kind of a bestial monster would the wolf consider man if it saw him in his slaughter-house killing thousands of innocent beef, sheep and hogs daily? Or what would it think of civilized man if it saw him shooting myriads of tame and harmless pigeons for amusement, or broiling lobsters alive to satisfy his gormandizing desires? Perhaps the wolf would set man below its grade, if interrogated upon the subject. But tyrannical man, intoxicated by his own egotism and clinging to an elastic religion which allows him to act as he pleases, feels that his god created all these things for his special benefit. If the wolf could be questioned about the matter, it too might claim that its god permitted the killing and eating of man. Mr. Porkpacker was considered both great and good by his fellow beings, for each year he gave thousands of dollars for the erection and maintenance of the church and likewise contributed largely toward his pastor's salary. Would it be good policy then for the pastor to believe that it was wrong to kill sheep, when one of the large contributors was earning money in that business? No, no. So the church upheld the slaughter-houses and proved by the scriptures that they were simply doing what the savages had done thousands of years previously according to divine right.

Once I listened to my father preach a sermon on the beautiful innocence and purity of the lamb. For an hour he spoke feelingly of the many virtues contained by this gentle little creature and after he was through he immediately went home and filled his stomach with roasted lamb for dinner. Good Christians are anxious to know when the time will arrive that the lion and lamb will lie down together in peace and harmony. Possibly the lamb would like to know if the time will ever come when its carcass will not be utilized to appease the voracious appetite of the Christian.

In looking over the so-called great business men and financial swindlers of America they certainly presented a motley collection of physical and mental monstrosities. They spent so much of their time in the mad rush for dollars and how to spend them, that physical and mental improvement received very little attention. Their brains became stagnant for the want of proper training and their bodies were allowed to rot and become useless for the need of exercise. Some were so fat they could not walk, while others were too lean to stand. A great many of them used either canes or crutches as an aid to hobble along or vehicles to convey them from place to place. Nearly all were cripples, more or less; rheumatism, gout, paralysis and numerous other ailments being the cause of their helplessness. Few of them seemed able to understand that all these infirmities were directly caused by the want of proper exercise and from the gluttonous habit of overloading their stomachs with foods of many kinds and meat especially. Apparently it was beyond their comprehension that nature commanded them to improve their physiques for the benefit of coming generations. Men who professed to be athletes when they were past the age of thirty were considered childish, while the exponents of physical culture were generally looked upon as cranks. Eating, drinking and smoking were adapted as the best modes of recreation, while fishing and shooting pigeons, quail, squirrels and other harmless living things were regarded as good, healthy amusements. Of all the brutal methods of diversion ever adopted by man, fishing is perhaps the most cruel. If the reader does not think so, just stop for a moment and imagine yourself being hooked to a great line by the mouth and your body being drawn far up into space and into another atmosphere, there to strangle slowly to death. You would not like it, would you? Then why should the fish be treated so? Do you not suppose that the fish have feelings like yourself? Oh, if all my fellowmen could only have taken that trip around the world with Arletta and seen things as I saw them, cruelty in all its various forms would be a thing of the past. That trip and my subsequent experience with her proved to be the best education I could have received from any source. It taught me the real meaning of the word kindness, without which, not only toward human beings, but toward all living things, man will never rise above the savage state.

CHAPTER X

We were just twenty-four hours making our journey around the world, when suddenly I found myself once more gazing into the beautiful eyes of Arletta. While she bestowed a kindly look of sympathy toward me, her features plainly showed that her gentle nature had received an awful shock from the terrible and degrading sights we had witnessed. And there was much reason why this pure and lovable woman should be shocked at what we had seen, for even I, a worthless and hardened vagabond, had become thoroughly disgusted with my own species.

"And what do you think of your highly civilized people now?" she inquired sadly. "They are a race of tail-less monkeys and filthy beasts with myself included," responded I, with vehemence, and then I began a tirade of abuse against the entire human family.

"Stop," exclaimed Arletta, "you must not allow malice to enter your mind against any living creature, no matter how beastly or brutal it may be. Hatred will not make the world better; it needs love. No living being is responsible for what it is any more than you or I are accountable for being in existence. But while each individual inherits the good or bad instincts of its predecessor, still it has the power to make better or worse its own condition. Love will not only make better your own condition, but that of your fellow beings as well. Do not expect to find in others that which you do not possess yourself. It is your duty to set a good example, not wait for others to accomplish what you have not done yourself. So begin right now with love. Cast away all unkind thoughts and never allow another to enter your mind, no matter what the provocation might be. I admit that the Apeman of today is no better, in fact, in many respects is much inferior to the Apeman who lived over four thousand years ago, but that is because he took the wrong road in trying to reach real manhood. He is still on the wrong path, but must be turned about and started in the right direction. He must be taught that Heaven is here on earth, if he will only make it so. But the earth will never be a paradise, so long as he allows a grain of selfishness to remain in his system. In yonder picture you can see what real men were like. Study their countenances carefully and see if you can read that any one of them ever committed a selfish act or even permitted an unkind thought to enter his mind, for if he had, you could plainly read it from his features, the face being the mirror of our thoughts and actions, and no matter what we do or what we think from the time we are born until we die, every act and thought is indelibly stamped upon our faces and can never be erased until the material of which we are composed has disintegrated and reentered the great chemical basin from which all living things receive their matter and energy. And it is to be hoped that with each turn of the chemical wheel the succeeding generation will be re-moulded on a better scale, until the Apeman and all lower animals have passed through a successful course of evolution and finally emerge into real manhood--the highest type of earthly beings. This goal is but a few steps and within the power of the Apeman to reach, but he must take his steps in the right direction. A whole nation of those magnificent beings you see in the picture, once existed in real life. Their ancestors were Apemen who were started in the right path, and after persistently sticking to the upward march of unselfish progress for many generations, ultimately reached the class of men you see before you; giants, physically, mentally and morally." And here she paused and looked long and affectionately at those wonderful figures in the painting. Then a feeling of intense jealousy suddenly crept into my brain, and I thought I would surely go mad under its terrible pressure. Arletta was in love with one of those real men, while she held merely a compassionate feeling for me.

I, the Apeman, standing six feet two inches in height and weighing over two hundred pounds avoirdupois, heretofore regarded as a marvel in physical development, now, in the presence of these eight-foot giants, felt like a shrunken pigmy. Formerly it was generally conceded that I was a rather handsome fellow. This woman thought I was hideous. Previously, I had felt proud of my nicely curled heavy black mustache, now I thought it made me look like a monkey. The splendid features of the real men were not disfigured by a hair or blemish of any kind, while their skin was as soft and smooth as that of a new born child. During my trip around the world, I had observed that the more man's body was covered by hair, the more ape-like he appeared, especially when decorating his face with it, and I was certain that my appearance was just as ludicrous in the eyes of Arletta as those I had seen. Therefore my admiration for the stately objects portrayed in the picture was beginning to turn into hatred. I inwardly wished they were alive that I might have an opportunity to combat with one or all of them in order to show Arletta that I possessed the courage to fight until death for her love. While lost in the midst of such reflections Arletta turned her gaze upon me fixedly and said: "What barbaric thoughts have you permitted to enter your mind now?" "I was wishing," replied I rather sullenly, "that the man you love in that picture was alive, that I might have the chance to demonstrate my worth in a fight to secure your favor; perhaps, then, you would discover that I had some good qualities."

"And do you suppose if I saw you fighting like a savage bulldog that I would admire those brutish tendencies in your nature?" inquired she. "Do you think that the animal instincts of fighting and killing are good qualities to possess? Has your trip around the world borne no good results? You have observed that your own species, like other savage beasts, quarrel, fight, maim and kill each other through selfish motives, and you have condemned them for it; now you would continue to do the very same thing yourself and think that I would consider it courageous. According to one of our primitive laws, the courageous man was he who feared no one and caused no one to fear him. These men of the picture were the bravest of the brave, and still if one of them were alive today he would not fight with you, no matter how much you might ill use him, for he would know that it required more real strength to take abuse than to give it. He would suffer more pain if he hurt you than if you injured him. And still he could have crushed you with greater ease than a cat can a mouse, if he were cowardly enough to do it. That is the real courage of unselfishness--the kind your species cannot understand. Your fellow beings applaud cowardice which they mistake for strength of character. They seem unable to comprehend that it requires far more courage to suffer pain than to inflict it upon others. They have inherited their erroneous ideas from the wild beasts who preceded them, and at the present time few of them know any better. But they must be taught differently and the teachers must set the examples, not merely offer advice. The different countries of the world today support large armies of licensed murderers who are commonly called soldiers. They are sent to the battle-fields to slaughter each other for selfish purposes. The strongest side is naturally victorious, and after killing as many of their adversaries as possible, return home to receive the applause and admiration of their countrymen. They are considered heroic because they were successful in slaying their weaker opponents. Your society worships these human butchers and the more lives one of them has destroyed the bigger the monument is erected in his honor. How many of these butchers would have the courage to take an insult from a weaker party without resenting it? It requires great bravery for the strong to refrain from taking advantage of the weak; it demands real heroism for the strong to equally share the results of their labors with the feeble. For the strong are doubly blessed in having strength while the weak are unfortunate and need sympathy."

"Would it not be courageous for one person to die for the love of another?" inquired I.

"That would depend altogether upon the circumstances," replied Arletta. "It would require far more courage to sacrifice your life for one you did not love as there would then be no selfish motive behind it. As I understand your feelings, you love me and imagine that you would not care to live without me."

"Yes," said I fervently, "I shall take my own life sooner than leave you."

"That is not courage at all, it is simply cowardice," answered she. "Through your own selfishness in trying to obtain something beyond your reach, you lack the strength to live without it. It takes far more courage to live when you want to die than to die when you want to live. Unselfishness is the very highest type of courageousness and one must live for the good he may do the world instead of his own personal aggrandizement. Thousands of our noble men sacrificed their lives yearly for the good of the world. Our laws permitted a certain number of them to leave their heavenly country periodically to go among the Apemen, and try and teach these barbarians the meaning of unselfish love. They never returned. They fully realized before starting on these missionary trips, that they were depriving themselves of all the luxuries the earth provided for a life of hardship and suffering; a life of insults and all the cruel tortures the ferocious Apemen could inflict upon them. But it pleased them to know that they possessed the courage to withstand all the insults heaped upon them, while trying to alleviate the conditions of others. Unlike your present missionaries they did not go into different countries backed up by loaded guns ready to annihilate all who did not believe their doctrines. If you hit a man on the head with a club and then tell him that you love him he will not believe you. They understood that to teach the Apemen to love one another they must set themselves up as examples, not with mere words, but by unselfish and courageous acts. They also knew that they had no divine right to enter another country and force upon the inhabitants their laws and customs. They merely went to teach their methods and in trying to do good for others were willing to accept insults in return for their kindness in order to prove their sincerity of purpose.

"At first, these good men were looked upon as gods by the Apemen who wished to worship them as such, and had they been vain-glorious like the Apeman himself, they would have allowed this false idea to exist. But no, there was not a grain of vanity or selfishness in their systems. They had not left their homes and friends to be worshiped, but had gone away to show the Apeman how he might reach real manhood, if he would but follow their instructions. They taught the eradication of selfishness from all living beings and the abolition of the system of individual accumulation, practiced then and now by all of your species. Of course when the rich and religious rulers of the different tribes and nations learned that these men were teaching that all living beings should have an equal chance in life, and that the weak should enjoy the same comforts as the strong, and that their divine right laws were unjust, they became wroth and ordered our men to be put to death by the most cruel methods. Some were burned at the stake; others were buried alive; several were put into dungeons and their bodies allowed to rot; many were cast into fiery furnaces, while a number of them were thrown into dens containing lions and tigers. All these tortures and innumerable others, did these brave men suffer that they might impress upon the Apeman the real meaning of courage and unselfishness. And through the power of mind sight we used to see these heroic volunteers unflinchingly suffer these indignities for the cause of righteousness, notwithstanding we had the power to annihilate the entire Apeman species, if we had so desired. Our chemists could have turned on currents of poisonous air and asphyxiated whole nations of them at once; our electricians could have sent an electric shock around the earth that would have left a path of destruction a thousand miles in width; our scientists could have concentrated the full force of the sun's rays upon any particular city they might choose and burn it up instantly; but they did not. We had the power to destroy, but the courage of forbearance. The highest honor our nation could bestow upon a man was to allow him to leave his heavenly country and become a martyr to his own unselfishness in trying to uplift the Apeman species. And had it not been for the unfortunate catastrophe which I shall explain to you later, our plans would have succeeded and the earth today would have been heaven with no such creature in existence as the Apeman."

CHAPTER XI

"Next to selfishness, religion has been the greatest drawback towards progress the Apeman has had to contend with in all ages," continued Arletta.

"Religion is the outgrowth of ignorance and the Apeman, just starting up the ladder of human knowledge, adopted it as an explanation of things of which he knew nothing. All religions were created by the Apeman; and wherein lies the difference between the god built of stone or from the imagination? In constructing the numberless religions, the Apeman invariably made them to suit his own habits and customs. He built his gods to please his own fancy and gave his own ideas as those of his deities. His own knowledge is likewise the extent of the wisdom contained by his gods, whom lie manufactured to be twisted and turned in any direction and made to answer any purpose he might see fit. No one religion is any worse than all the rest. They are all founded on ignorance, superstition and selfishness. To believe in any of these petty religions is to cast insults upon the real Creator of the universe, for a god created by the Apeman must naturally be a very inferior being. Each devout worshiper can point out the errors and absurdities of every other religion excepting his own. He is capable of utilizing his reasoning powers until directed against himself, and narrowed down to a few words he feels that he is all right but everybody else is all wrong. Of the several hundred religions now extant, would it not be more reasonable to suppose that they were all wrong than to believe they were all right? Take your own religion for instance; you are worshiping a most unnatural god. In fact your Bible puts him in the position of a vain-glorious tyrant. According to the Bible an Apeman can be no worse than his god no matter how bad he may be. The main reason why. the Apeman believes in religion is because he is an inveterate coward and fears some dire punishment if he investigates the matter. But believe me, if the Creator gave you the power to reason, he certainly will not condemn you for making use of your reasoning faculties in not accepting opinions which appear untenable. So let us look into this matter from an impartial point of view. In the first place the offer of rewards for doing good, which is the foundation of all religions is wrong, for it carries selfishness right to the very gates of the imaginary heavens. Goodness is very shallow indeed if it cannot exist without rewards being offered for it. I shall enumerate a few things your god was supposed to have said or allowed, according to the Bible, which would make no Apeman living, any worse in his moral conduct.

"Enmity.--'And I will put enmity between thee and the woman.' Gen. iii, 15.

"Unkindness.--'Unto the woman He said, I will greatly multiply thy sorrow.' Gen. iii, 16.

"Flesh Eaters.--'Every moving thing that liveth shall be meat for you.' Gen. ix, 3.

"Revenge.--'Whoso sheddeth man's blood, by man shall his blood be shed.' Gen. ix, 6.

"Drunkenness.--'And he drank of the wine, and was drunken.' Gen. ix, 21.

"Partiality.--'God shall enlarge Japheth, and he shall dwell in the tents of Shem and Canaan shall be his servant.' Gen. ix, 27.

"Hunting--'He was a mighty hunter before the Lord.' Gen. x, 9.

"A curser.--'And I will bless them that bless thee, and curse them that curseth thee.' Gen. xii, 3.

"Fraud.--'By fraud, Jacob received the blessing intended for Esau and then God blessed him and made him prosperous forever afterward. Gen. xxvii to xxix.

"Fornication.--'And Bilhah, Rachel's maid, conceived again and bare Jacob a second son.' Gen. xxx, 7.

"Anger.--'And the anger of the Lord was kindled against Moses.' Exodus iv, 14.

"Thievery.--'Speak now into the ears of the people and let every man borrow of his neighbor and every woman of her neighbor jewels of silver and jewels of gold.' Exodus xi, 2.

"Carnage.--'For I will pass through the land of Egypt this night and will smite all the first born in the land of Egypt, both man and beast; and against all the gods of Egypt I will execute judgment; I am the Lord.' Exodus xii, 12.

"Jealousy.--'For I the Lord thy God am jealous God.' Exodus xx, 5.

"Slavery.--'Then his master shall bring him unto the judges; he shall also bring him to the door, or unto the doorpost, and his master shall bore his ear through with an awl; and he shall serve him forever.' Exodus xxi, 6.

"Witchcraft.--'Thou shalt not suffer a witch to live.' Exodus xxii, 18.

"Murder.--'And my wrath shall wax hot, and I will kill you with my sword and your wives shall be widows and your children fatherless.' Exodus xxii, 24.

"Changeability.--'And the Lord spake unto Moses, saying, Phinehas, the son of Eleazar, the son of Aaron the priest, hath turned my wrath away from the children of Israel, while he was zealous for my sake among them, that I consumed not the children of Israel in my jealousy.' Numbers xxv, 10, 11.

"Brutality.--'And the Lord spake unto Moses, saying, Bring forth him that hath cursed without the camp; and let all that heard him lay their hands upon his head, and let all the congregation stone him.' Leviticus xxiv, 13, 14.

"Savage Cruelty.--'And if the burnt sacrifice for his offering to the Lord be of fowls, then he shall bring his offering of turtle doves, or of young pigeons. And the priest shall bring it unto the altar, and wring off its head, and burn it on the altar; and the blood thereof shall be wrung out at the ides of the altar.' Leviticus i, 14, 15.

"An Ass.--'And the Lord opened the mouth of the ass and she said unto Balaam, What have I done unto thee that thou hast smitten me these three times?' Numbers xxii, 28.

"I have brought a few of these absurd writings to your attention," said Arletta, "hoping that later on you will go over them carefully and give them the same rational consideration you bestow upon other subjects. There is one commendable feature about your Bible however, and that is, it shows that once there existed among your species a noble mortal who devoted his life trying to teach the Apeman human kindness in somewhat the same manner our men used to do, with the exception of the supernatural dogmas. I refer to Jesus Christ. The fact that the same lessons he expounded were taught thousands of years before he was born, or that he failed to grasp nature's beautiful ideas without confounding them with supernatural fancies, does not detract in any way from his nobility of purpose and his name should be mentioned in the future history of the world as one of the great benefactors of the human race. It seems a pity that his over-zealous followers have tried to place him in the light of a deity, for in time to come, when your species begin to reason, they might possibly regard him as an impostor. This should not be the case however, for although Christ no doubt really believed in a religious god, it is unjust to believe that he ever pretended to be anything more than a mere human being himself, or that he knew anything about the wonderful miracles it was subsequently claimed he had performed.

"Any earthly being," said Arletta, as her face fairly beamed with intelligence, "whether it be a man, an Apeman or a monkey, who claims to be related to the Creator of the universe, or to be His prophet, or His specially appointed spokesman, or in any way tries to lead others to believe that he possesses supernatural powers, is either an impostor or an idiot.

"When all earthly beings make use of the reasoning faculties nature endows them with, all religions will perish through the agency of their own untruths."

CHAPTER XII

"Then am I to understand that your people were Atheists?" inquired I of Arletta.

"Not at all," replied she. "We believed in Natural Law but not in religion. Our most intellectual men decided that by no stretch of the imagination could they build a god for religious purposes as great as the Creator of the universe must naturally be, and knowing that it remains for man himself to reach his highest state of perfection without any supernatural influence whatsoever, they therefore abolished all forms of religious worship and established a code of ethics which was termed Natural Law.

"Religion teaches one to believe in an unnatural god who apparently must be ever ready to answer anybody's prayerful cry and act as a general servant to humanity by distributing good things to those who beg for them; a sort of meddlesome god who enters into all the petty quarrels of hunan beings and generally settles them in the wrong way.

"Natural Law teaches that there exists on grand supreme ruler who guides the entire machinery of the universe; the Deity who created the principle of life, and one who does not deviate from His eternal and immutable laws; an all-wise, everlasting and unchangeable being far beyond the faintest conception the brain of man has ever been able to formulate. His power unlimited; His laws supreme; His goodness incalculable.

"Natural Law explains that He created the principle from which humanity evolved, but that it remains for all living things to make better or worse their own conditions. His laws may be studied and practiced by all human beings, but to claim to know the reasons of the

Creator's actions would be to assume His wisdom and knowledge. His purposes, therefore, are unfathomable.

"Natural Law sets forth that notwithstanding the earth is but a mere speck in the universe, still, it being a part of the vast machinery governed by the Almighty, there is a reason for its existence and a work for it to perform. Like other bodies in space, it contains particles of living matter which are constantly passing through a course of development with methodical changes from life to death and from death to life. But while all living things live and die, the material thereof is used over and over again indefinitely. Human beings are a species of these particles. All living things are composed of three parts, matter, energy and soul. The matter is the machinery; energy the motion and soul the engineer. The mind is that part of the machinery having power to control its movements. The soul is the spark of life and acts as a moral guide to the mind. Soul and conscience are synonymous. The soul, always pure, is continually striving to improve the condition of the mind. The mind alone is responsible for the disposition of the body and the evils arising therefrom, the soul merely acting as its instructor for good. It is the mind which inherits evil instincts and but for the good influence of the soul, living creatures would not exist in harmony. As the mind hardens against righteousness the sway of the soul is lessened, but as the mind softens towards goodness the soul increases its power. There is a continual struggle between the soul for good and the mind for evil, but the soul will eventually gain the ascendancy and all living things will be cleansed of impurities.

"The body, including the mind, of each living thing dies, the material disintegrates and passes into the composition of other forms. The soul never dies; it remains in one body until its collapse and then transmigrates into another. The soul of man today may be that of a lower animal tomorrow; therefore he should use the greatest kindness and consideration toward all living things. There is only a certain quantity of matter upon earth to be moulded together in living forms and a certain number of souls to abide therein, so that with the increase of mankind there must naturally be a decrease in the ranks of other animals, hence it remains the duty of man to extend in number and quality his own species until all the material in existence is utilized by human beings of the very highest intelligence. Humanity, however, will never rise above the savage state until the barbarous custom of killing and eating other animals is abolished.

"Selfishness is the root of all evil; eradicate selfishness from humanity and the earth will be heaven.

"Man's heaven is here on earth if he is only capable of making it so, but men cannot enjoy heavenly blessings with hellish minds, and no selfish being can properly enjoy the sweets of life. The real essence and pleasure of life can only be extracted when mankind labors harmoniously together as a unit, instead of each individual struggling separately and murderously to obtain the largest portion of the earth's blessings. The production of the world must be divided equally among all honest toilers and man's greatest happiness must arise from serving others instead of himself. No good mortal can thoroughly enjoy luxuries that are beyond the reach of his fellow men, therefore all human beings should work together as one; enjoying equally the fruits of their combined efforts; the weak and the strong alike. There must be but one master--the entire human race bound together as one. When mankind, acting as a unit, masters itself, then will it rule the earth and gain knowledge of extraneous matters; thus the wisdom of inhabitants of older and more advanced worlds will be attained and intercourse with them practiced, thereby unraveling many apparent mysteries of the universe.

"It is an error to suppose that the Deity is your maker; He created the source from which all living things sprung, but collectively, man makes himself and is responsible for his own conditions. If the Almighty was your maker then the production of criminals, cripples and lunatics would demonstrate very bad workmanship, so do not try to shift the blame for human weakness upon the Creator of the universe. The Deity controls the principle of life; man controls himself.

"Do not pray; you cannot alter the Creator's plans and you place him in the light of a petty vanity seeker when claiming that he wants to be worshipped. Better please the Omnipotent by kind acts toward all living creatures than by offering ridiculous exhortations for favors and forgiveness. You proffer insults to the Creator when you claim you can change His immutable plans by prayer; when you think he would take from one and give to another; when you pretend to communicate with Him; when you imagine He takes part in the silly squabbles of human beings; when you say that man was made in His image; when you take His name in vain.

"A united world, with all living things on the same plane of perfection and working harmoniously together for the common good is the heaven humanity should strive to reach. It is within the power of mankind to perfect itself, but this can only be accomplished through the unselfish efforts of the whole people. Each individual can make better or worse his own condition and thereby stamp a good or bad impression upon the lives of his descendants. The creature who passes his life without adding to the knowledge and goodness of the world has lived for naught, and he who fails to improve his own worth morally, mentally or physically has spent a life of uselessness for which his descendants must suffer; for to misuse oneself is to commit a crime against posterity. Each generation should be an improvement upon the preceding one. Having been entrusted with a piece of living machinery, it is the duty of everyone to give it the very best care and attention possible, that its value might be increased to nature, hence moral, mental and physical perfection are the highest aims of life to achieve. Parents should have no off-spring when one or both of them are insane, diseased, gluttons, drunkards or criminals.

"Practice moderation in all things that you may live longer and acquire strength to enjoy natural blessings and bestow character upon those to follow. Pleasure can only be extracted from temperateness; it increases or decreases in proportion to quantity, and he who takes sparingly, lives longer to enjoy the most. Do not over-work, over-study, over-eat, over-drink, over-sleep, or commit any excess whatsoever. The surest way to make the world better is to begin with yourself. Such is the essence of Natural Law."

CHAPTER XIII

"At the present time," proceeded Arletta, "the earth resembles a huge table over-loaded with good things and surrounded by a pack of gluttons each striving to secure the largest portion. And in this piggish scramble the strong obtain more and the weak less than is needed while enough is wasted to amply supply the whole. The best forces of the participants, which should be utilized for other purposes are also lost in the ravenous struggle, for it requires more power to retain than obtain these things.

"The same avaricious principal--individual accumulation--is the foundation of every government in the world today, and consequently all of your social systems are being run upside down. Your people spend their time and strength in looking for remedies instead of stopping the source from which all evils flow. Corruption is the result of a diseased root and as long as that remains, iniquities will continue to multiply. Extirpate the cause, however, and sin will depart like magic.

"The system which allows the individual to acquire personal wealth is the direct cause for nearly every evil in existence. There is no remedy for a wrong unless you eradicate it entirely, and just as long as a nation clings to the pernicious plan which permits separate persons to store up the products of the earth for private uses, just so long will selfishness be the characteristic feature of the people, and all kinds of criminals will be bred from the material which otherwise would prove very useful to a unified world. According to present methods success is based upon what each individual accumulates and not what mankind is capable of producing.

"The foundation of existence is effort, without which the inhabitants of the world would perish. United exertion produces better results and with less toil than competitive efforts. With united labor in force, every living being must work, for he who consumes and does not produce is a thief. If all the inhabitants of the world combined their labors on the most economic basis, there would be enough comforts for all created by one-tenth of the power expended at the present time. Each person would add his mite to the whole, and in return would receive as much as anyone else. All worthless occupations would be done away with, and the power thereof directed into useful channels. Labor would rule the world instead of money. For of what good would be all the money on earth if there was no labor to produce the necessities of life? At present there exists but one honest toiler whose labors enrich the world, to ten schemers who spend their time plotting to secure the results of his work; and these parasites actually confiscate the largest portion of that which is produced. The schemers feast and govern, while the laborers fast and are governed. Can you imagine more unnatural conditions than one class of beings producing all the comforts and receiving none in return?

"With the abolition of the noxious system of individual accumulation, money would have no value and all the evils arising therefrom would cease. Take away the opportunity of the individual to accumulate wealth for himself, and you remove the temptation for fraud, theft and numerous other crimes, for there is then no incentive left for them. Expel the motive and selfishness will disappear, and each mortal give his best efforts toward perfecting himself morally, mentally and physically for the good he may render the world.

"Teach the child that it will not have to worry over the future; that it will not have to lie, cheat, steal, murder or take any advantage of its fellow beings in order to receive its share of the good things of life; explain to it that the real incentive is to give its best services toward increasing the general production of the earth, that all mankind may enjoy the sweets thereof together in peace and harmony; impress upon its young mind, that he who works in excess of others for the good of mankind, lives the noblest life and receives the highest esteem of his fellow beings and the blessed approbation of his own soul, and that child, reaching maturity, will be a thousand times more useful to himself and humanity than he who has been taught to hoard up riches for his own special purposes.

"Individual accumulation is responsible for crime; crime necessitates laws; laws breed tyranny.

"Abolish individualism, and crime, tyranny and nine-tenths of your superfluous laws will be exterminated.

"A few well-defined and just laws properly enforced are sufficient to successfully operate the governmental machinery of the human race according to Natural Law."

CHAPTER XIV

"Telepathy," continued Arletta, "proved to be one of the greatest factors for good utilized by our people. Through its agency we not only found that it was the most natural and complete way to converse with one another, but also learned to think collectively as well as singly.

"The brain is both a receiver and transmitter of thought, and all minds are directly connected with each other by an invisible force. Thought is an element of life and exists everywhere; it is not originated by the mind, but is a utility for it. Thoughts are sustenance for the brain, as air is for the lungs, or food for the appetite; they are good and bad in quality, and it is within man's power to accept or reject them at will. By admitting good and repelling bad thoughts, the brain acquires moral as well as mental strength but vice versa it is poisoned, and degeneracy is sure to follow.

"Nature created both the mountains and the thoughts; look and you can see those lofty hills; think and you can receive inspiring thoughts. Shut your eyes and you cannot see; close your brain and you cannot think. The broader the mind, the greater the ideas to enter. Ignorance is bred from a closed brain; intelligence from an open one. He who is incapable of thinking is like the blind who cannot see or the deaf who cannot hear. The thought is the mightiest force for good or evil, humanity has to contend with; time is measured by it and pure meditation makes the days short and sweet, while evil notions lengthen and depreciate them. The mind that retains good ideas and refuses bad ones is of incalculable value to mankind for it has an instantaneous effect upon other minds in all parts of the earth.

"It is easier for many minds working in harmony together to grasp a thought, than for the single brain to receive it without aid. No one earthly being ever conceived a great idea unassisted. One might have believed and proclaimed the origin of an idea, but unknown and innumerable others secretly aided in its conception. The strongest intellect, however, retained and gave it to the world, and he who accepts, practices and impresses the thought upon others, deserves the credit thereof.

"It took several generations of continuous experimentation by the Sagemen to acquire the fundamental principles of telepathy and many more to establish the custom of conversing with the mind instead of the voice. In the beginning, the evil ones looked upon the practice with horror, for it was impossible to conceal anything from their fellow beings. But this very fact alone caused them to keep clean and allow no impure thoughts to enter their minds that would lower them in the estimation of their associates, and after a few generations of active use it was accepted as one of the great benefits of nature.

"Whenever a great problem confronted the nation, a hundred or more of our deepest thinkers would simultaneously concentrate their mental forces upon it, and if unsuccessful in reaching a satisfactory conclusion, then the whole people would devote an hour each day upon it until finally solved. Thus in thought as well as in action we labored together as a unit, harmoniously working out vast ideas that never could have been conceived by a single brain, and each mortal receiving an equal share of the many blessings derived therefrom.

"And there again is where your individual system retards natural progress. A little Apeman receives part of one of nature's ideas. His immature brain is incapable of receiving the whole of it so he spends his entire life stumbling along in the dark, vainly searching for the remainder. Sometimes he becomes insane or dies under the strain of the burden, and mankind loses the portion he had already understood. It was his greedy desire that caused him to struggle alone for something that many minds could easily have brought forth had they been called to his assistance. But no, his purpose was not to aid humanity, but get money and the power to wield over his fellow creatures by accepting and having patented for himself one of nature's gifts.

"And then again one of your little Apemen finally does conceive a good idea, or part of one, after thirty years, more or less, of constant strain upon his mental faculties. So the progress of the world must be held in check for that length of time for an invention that could have been produced and put into useful operation by the combined efforts of many minds in a few days, weeks or months. But it is the individual system and not the individual himself which causes this stupendous waste of time and power, and as long as it is kept in force the leakage of human progress will naturally be beyond calculation.

"It seems a pity," said Arletta, looking at me sympathetically, "that your brain is not sufficiently developed to enable you to grasp the magnificent principle of life as it was understood by the Sage-men, but it would be as hard for you to comprehend an attempted explanation of the whole subject as it would be for a monkey to understand algebra. So I have to be content with impressing upon your little intellect just as much as it will absorb.

"But come, you look tired, let us partake of some refreshments. And remember, do not overload your stomach."

CHAPTER XV

"Do not overload your stomach." This admonition caused me to feel like a child once more, and I was uncertain whether I ought to laugh or become indignant over the remark. Still I fully realized the necessity of this warning; not only for myself alone, but for the entire human race from which I sprung. How many beings are there in the world today who would not profit by following this advice? How many are there with sense enough to heed it? I cannot recall to memory any person I have ever met who had absolute control of his appetite.

"We take pleasure in living, but do not live for pleasure," continued Arletta, as she touched an invisible spring concealed within a dainty flower and graciously invited me to eat--or rather to breathe. And as I inhaled the delicious fumes it seemed that the very breath of life itself was injected into every pore of my body.

"That is enough of the soup," commented Arletta mirthfully, "now try the roast; now the entree; and here, perhaps, a little dessert will not hurt you; there, that is plenty; a little is strengthening but too much is poisonous.

"You see, this process of living is very simple indeed; our chemists merely extracted the vital parts of vegetables, herbs, cereals, fruits, nuts, flowers, etc., and reduced them to aeriform. These artificial flowers are arranged to conceal small tubes from which the nutriment flows. By operating these automatic springs the substance is allowed to escape in such quantities as is required for meals. Very simple, is it not? Much cleaner and better than munching a piece of fat pork, don't you think? And there are no cooks needed to prepare it, no waiters to serve it, nor any dishes to wash afterward. Our food was arranged ready for consumption at the great national laboratories and piped directly to the people, to use as they pleased."

"It is all very wonderful," exclaimed I, looking up to Arletta as if she were the goddess of life itself, "but there is one thing in particular I am anxious to know and that is: what causes daylight here when darkness prevails on the outside of this building?"

"Very simple," explained she, "about a thousand years before the great catastrophe our scientists discovered a method whereby they could store up the rays of the sun for light, heat and power, and after much experimenting they found that they could mix these rays with other ingredients into solid substances. The light you observed in the hallway before entering here is merely compressed into the material of which the walls are composed and as long as that remains light will shine from it. The light in this room comes from the miniature sun you see in the picture; that too will give forth radiance as long as the material holds together. Our scientists were remarkable men; they not only made use of the sun's rays in many different ways for the benefit of mankind, but actually controlled the power of the sun itself insofar as it related to the earth. They also restrained the atmosphere which surrounds the earth and made the weather conditions to suit their own welfare. But these things are so infinitely beyond the Apeman's comprehension, who feels that he has almost reached the limit of human resources with his crude little steam engines, that it would only be a waste of time and power to try and explain them to you, besides being a considerable strain upon your half-grown brain."

"This is certainly a wonderful painting," said I, looking about the room with much admiration. "I have never seen anything to compare with it before."

"There is nothing about it that is extraordinary," remarked Arletta, "it is merely a little ornamentation of my own private apartment which I did myself according to my own fancy. Any of our ordinary house decorators could have done as well or better. All of our children were taught to paint and they devoted considerable of their spare time to the art, but the works of the real artists were placed upon exhibition in the national galleries where everybody could see and enjoy their magnificence."

"I observe an absence of jewelry about your person," mentioned I, "was it not the custom of your people to wear jewels?"

"Do you think that to wear rings around your toes and suspended from your nose is a sensible thing to do?" inquired Arletta.

"No, no; decidedly not," answered I, "such are the customs of the barbarians only, but our civilized people wear rings around their fingers and in their ears."

"Indeed, and wherein lies the difference?" asked she, good naturedly. It then struck me rather forcibly that there was no difference and that it was just as ridiculous to wear rings from the ears and around the fingers as it was to have them suspended from the nose and about the toes. "But were there no diamonds in your country?" questioned I.

"Yes," replied Arletta, "there was a large pile of them in the national museum which we looked upon as old junk--sort of relics of the savage Apemen. When our children were shown these things and informed that a king of an Apeman nation would gladly sacrifice the lives of a hundred thousand of his subjects in an attempt to gain possession of them, or that his subjects would murder their friends, brothers, wives or children in an effort to secure some for themselves, it was impossible for their youthful minds to fully understand why the Apeman should become so ferocious and idiotic over such trifles. They naturally looked upon your species as you would view a tribe of monkeys fighting amongst themselves for the possession of a string of glass beads. The Apeman like the monkey is incapable of seeing his own absurdities."

"And what about gold?" I inquired. "We had a building constructed of it," answered she. "One of the first things the Sagemen did after they abolished the system of individual accumulation was to take all the gold there was in the country, and mould it into a huge edifice to be used as a national museum, and represent a sort of monument to a dead system."

"It must have been a magnificent structure," said I, in amazement. "On the contrary," replied Arletta, "it was the most hideous building in our land. As a curiosity it was worth seeing, but as an object of grandeur it was a total failure. There is more real beauty in one of nature's tiniest flowers than there would be in a mountain built of gold and studded with diamonds, but the little Apeman who considers gold the standard of value cannot understand this."

"When you mentioned the absurdity of wearing jewelry," said I, "it brought to my attention the fact that you wear no shoes upon your feet, and that your toes are much longer and far more shapely and supple than is the case nowadays."

"Yes," answered she, "that is because we made use of our toes as well as our fingers for useful purposes. It appears to me that the Apeman has permitted his feet to grow into mere hoofs with which to stump along upon, and from what I observed during my excursion around the world, your people are even allowing their hoofs to become worthless," and here she smiled as she recalled to mind some of the gouty, rheumatic and over-fed mortals she had seen during that trip.

As Arletta smiled, her beautiful lips parted and for the first time I noticed, much to my surprise, that she had no teeth. A woman of our own kind without teeth generally presents a rather dilapidated appearance, but here was a woman that I thought actually looked more lovely without them.

"Well," remarked Arletta, noting my astonishment, "I do not have teeth to bite and chew with like the lower animals. The Sageman shed his teeth shortly after he discontinued the filthy animal habit of devouring flesh and other solid substances for subsistence, and substituted the more scientific, cleanly and healthful method of inhalation."

CHAPTER XVI

"Now we shall enjoy a little music," said Arletta, as she turned her attention to the pictorial orchestra.

"Music," repeated I, "then it was real music I heard a short time ago and not a mere fancy of my own."

"I was not aware that you heard it at all," replied she. "Yes," responded I, "when first coming into this room, the men in the picture appeared to me to be alive, and wishing to attract their attention I touched the shoulder of the leader, and then it was that I thought I heard the sweetest and grandest music it has ever been my good fortune to listen to."

"In that case," said Arletta, "your ears did not deceive you, for you certainly heard real music. You see in this picture, an exact portrayal of that which existed over four thousand years ago. This delineation is an almost perfect representation of one of our national bands as they once appeared in life ready to play. The music, of course, is reproduced mechanically, the mechanism being concealed from view behind the scenery. When you placed your hand upon the shoulder of the leader you unconsciously pressed the spring which set the machinery in motion, causing a reproduction of the same strains once rendered by these men."

"But this being a painting, I cannot understand how the figures moved as if playing upon their instruments," said I.

"They did not move at all," answered Arletta, "it was your soul that brought to your senses the movements that once took place among these men in real life. Music is inspired by the soul, and likewise has a direct influence upon it. No Sageman was considered an eminent composer if his work lacked the force to convey the soul of the listener to the actual scene from whence the inspiration was derived. No doubt your inferior brain was incapable of grasping the magnificent conception of the author, but the selection being so enrapturous your soul awakened and brought your senses to the point where you could see the movements of the musicians. Perhaps the next rendition may have a stronger effect upon your soul which will cause you to get an outline of what was intended by the composer. The composition which the orchestra will now reproduce for your benefit was considered by our people to be the musical masterpiece of all time. It was named 'The Soul's Retrospection,' and was composed by the leader of this band only a few years prior to the great catastrophe. Look," said Arletta, with much feeling as she waved her hand toward the exalted director, "take a good look at this model of a perfect man and you may be able to realize just what qualities he had to possess before acquiring the tremendous intellectual strength necessary to produce the wonderful work that will shortly be impressed upon you. Note the extraordinary look of kindness, gentleness and self-denial that is stamped upon his handsome features. See the expression of thankfulness and intense reverence he maintained for the many splendid gifts nature bestows upon all mankind capable of accepting them. Observe the optimistic appearance of one that believed the earth was real heaven and who strived to make it so. Notice the cast of superior intellectuality caused by devoting his time and mentality to natural thoughts, instead of allowing absurd civilized theories to take root in his expansive brain. Behold the magnificent physique, the result of the constant care and attention he gave to the machinery nature provided him with. Ah, me! such a noble being, and to think that there is not another piece of flesh and blood on earth at the present time to compare with him seems cruel."

At this point Arletta appeared almost overcome with sadness and emotion as she buried herself in contemplation of a glorious past and an unknown future. Great tears rolled from her beautiful eyes, and unconsciously from my own as well. How utterly helpless I felt at that moment. I knew of no way to cheer her, although I would have gladly given up my life to do so. Aye, more than that, my love for her was so strong that in order to make her happy, I should have welcomed back to life again, if such a thing were possible, any one of those handsome fellows in the picture. However, by a superb display of will power, she quickly regained control of herself, and becoming cheerful once more, bade me recline upon one of the lounges while she pressed the spring which set the musical apparatus in motion.

And as I followed her directions, there suddenly burst forth the voluminous and harmonious sound of a hundred strange instruments, causing an indescribable thrill of ecstasy to take possession of my senses, until it seemed that there was nothing left of me but an invisible spirit. And then, even the music apparently stopped, and a peculiar feeling overcame me as if my soul had actually left its charge and was flying about in an effort to find a convenient resting place. Suddenly, as if half awake and half dreaming, I found myself within a luxuriously furnished hall, surrounded by a score of richly-clad beings, who were bowing, kneeling, and cutting up all sorts of silly antics about me. In a dreamy sort of a way, I looked down at myself and discovered that I was arrayed in the gorgeous garments of a king, and weighted down with dazzling jewels from head to foot. Then everything became clear enough to my memory; I was the king, and these idiotic creatures fawning and cringing about me were my obedient subjects; my slaves; the willing tools which kept me in power. A gouty feeling in my feet, a dyspeptic ache of the stomach and an alcoholic pain in the head, caused me to be in a very disagreeable mood, and I felt like kicking the entire gathering out of my presence.

"Sire," squeaked a knock-kneed, sickly looking civilized creature about five feet high, who wore knee breeches, silk stockings and fancy ribbons, as he bowed low in addressing me, "those ungrateful subjects of your majesty, the ignorant common laboring horde whom God in His infinite wisdom has entrusted to your noble guidance, have become dissatisfied and turbulent again, and are disturbing the peaceful prosperity of the domain by clamoring for bread--more bread and less toil is their beastly cry. A delegation of their representatives requested me to beg your majesty to grant them an audience that they might state their imaginary grievances to you in person."

"More bread and less toil," shouted I furiously, "the audacity of the vermin! By the gods! I shall teach those craven beggars that I am the master and will tolerate no new-fangled ideas. Give orders to the generalissimo to have this delegation beheaded at once and to put to the sword every dissatisfied laborer in the land." As I uttered those words, intermingled with terrible oaths, and with intense hatred for the wretches who dared to complain against such conditions a sudden change affected me and I found myself within a dark, filthy little room, seated at a bare table, with a feeling of hunger gnawing at my stomach. My limbs felt tired and sore from a hard day's toil. Beside me sat a thin, haggard, sorrowful woman and several half-famished children piteously crying for something to eat. Oh, what a dismal, melancholy feeling. "What is it," mused I, observing my bony hands, crooked limbs and ragged clothes, "that causes my inability to earn enough money to supply bread for myself and family, after working fifteen hours a day, while thousands of men in this land do not work at all and have luxuries to waste? What unnatural law governs the world that starves myself and family who work, and over-feeds the pet dog of the aristocrat, who loafs? The Church teaches me that God rules the universe, and that in order to please Him I must be contented with my lot. Can I believe this unreasonable doctrine of the Church? Can I give thanks to such a god?"

Another change, and behold, I am clad in the garments of a hunter, seated upon the back of a spirited horse and in mad pursuit of a fleet-footed antelope. I raise my rifle and blaze away at the frightened beast. There, I have hit the mark and brought him down at the first shot, much to my delight. But lo, it is not dead yet; see how it pants and struggles in desperation, as it tries to regain its feet. Now I am right upon it, and quickly dismounting, I take hold of its horns, draw a long keen knife from its sheath, and with a powerful stroke I almost sever the victim's head from the body. And as the warm blood pours forth in every direction and the last sign of life departs from its shivering body, I view the work of destruction with the fiendish glee of a noble sportsman.

But hold! What causes me to tremble with fear as though some blood-thirsty monster were pursuing me with the intention of crushing out my life's blood? Ah, I understand. I am the four-footed beast and am running, running, running as fast as my weary limbs will carry me. And such a terrified feeling overcomes me as I look backward and discover I am pursued by the most dangerous, savage and cruel animal in existence-- man. How relentlessly he dogs my footsteps. On, on, on he comes until he is right behind me and there is no chance to escape--nor any hope for quarter. At last being brought to bay I turn about and decide to give battle to my pursuer. But look! The cowardly savage will not fight after all. No, he will not advance and fight fair, but at a distance and out of harm's way, he stops, and pointing a weapon at me, takes deliberate aim, there is a loud report, a quick flash, and the scene once more changes.

And thus I transmigrated from one thing into another, in a seemingly endless procession of lives, experiencing all the peculiar sensations of the many bodies I temporarily inhabited. In some cases I was the big strong brute--either physically or mentally--taking advantage of the puny weakling. In others, I was the miserable weakling, being crushed by the over-powering strength of the bully. But whether strong or weak, either physically or mentally, I was always the moral coward and selfish creature, ready to cater to those who were stronger, and take advantage of those who were feebler than myself, until finally I emerged into a most extraordinary being, utterly deficient in all human weaknesses.

Master of a physique absolutely free from all imperfections, and controlling a mind powerful enough to grasp nature's beautiful ideas unadulterated, I found myself seated upon a platform in the center of a mammoth theatre and surrounded by the finest body of musicians the earth has ever produced--the immortal Sixth National Band of Sageland. Then I fully realized that as leader of this wonderful group I was about to render for the first time, my latest musical conception and masterpiece--"The Soul's Retrospection"--which would prove to humanity beyond a doubt, the positive truth of one of nature's grandest secrets--the indestructibility of the soul.

It was generally believed that music was the direct inspiration of the soul. It was also thought that the soul was one of the unchangeable forces of nature whose duty it was to operate and purify different pieces of natural machinery known as animal lives; starting each on its brief career and remaining a part thereof until the mechanism exhausted its power and collapsed, after which it attached itself to another bit of animal matter, remaining therewith until its death, and so on indefinitely.

And now, after a life of unswerving devotion to this purpose, I was about to establish the truth of these theories by producing a musical composition that would cause the listener's soul to leave the body, and going backward, revisit, as in a dream, the various animal forms it had previously inhabited. How extremely happy I felt to think what a great blessing humanity was about to receive direct from nature, through the instrumentality of myself and the incalculable good that would result therefrom. Not only would it prove of vast scientific value to my own countrymen, but also to the millions of ferocious Apemen in all parts of the world, who could now be made to understand that no soul is immune from hardship, misery and torture until all living things on earth have reached the highest stage of perfection.

The news that the first production of "The Soul's Retrospection" was about to be given had attracted great attention among the Sagemen, and I observed that the great National Auditorium, which was capable of seating four hundred thousand persons, was crowded to its very doors, a proceeding I had never witnessed before, notwithstanding my companions and I had appeared there many times previously to give musical performances. I also noticed that the transmitters in all of the domes of the auditorium were open and ready for use and I knew that my countrymen in every part of Sageland were at their musical receivers ready to obtain the instantaneous results of our efforts. All of the celebrated wise men and great scientists, while openly skeptical concerning the claims of my composition, showed their interest in the matter by being present personally and appearing anxious for success to crown my efforts. As my eyes wandered over the great assemblage completely filling tiers upon tiers of seats, as far back in every direction as the natural eye could reach, I felt positive that there was at least one person present who had no doubts of successful results. "Ah, where is she?" mused I, looking about for a sign of recognition. "Here I am," came the quick telepathic response, and immediately my gaze fell upon the loveliest woman on earth--Arletta--nature's companion to my soul. I am utterly powerless to describe the feeling of joy experienced as our eyes met in mutual admiration. Being held momentarily spellbound by her loving glance, I fully recognized the fact that she was the acme of purity--the guiding star of my life. And with such a guide there was no such thing as fail.

All in readiness, I arose to my feet and the entire audience did likewise, as a token of appreciation for past services rendered. Acknowledging the honor and waiving them seated, without further ado I signaled my assistants to begin.

Never did a body of musicians commence a difficult task with more determination to create, through the medium of their instruments, an exact interpretation of the author's purpose. In no degree could they have succeeded more admirably than on this occasion. Never was an entire audience so completely carried beyond the borders of reality than now. From the first until the last note not a twitch of a muscle could be seen in all that mass of humanity, which now resembled a great concourse of motionless statues. The musicians themselves, with their minds and souls bent upon giving the fullest expression to their grand work, were the only evidence that any life at all remained in the large auditorium. How bravely they stuck to their laborious undertaking; how beautifully they executed their divine work.

At last the piece was finished, and looking about, I observed that the great audience jumped to its feet instantly, and every person present frantically extended both hands above the head--a sign that we had been successful. Never before did I see my countrymen under such intense excitement and jubilation as now. Men hugged each other; women cried with joy. The world is saved, was the general exclamation. Amid the great confusion that followed, I noticed Arletta with her arms outstretched toward me--a sign that she was betrothed to me forever. Her beautiful face was the picture of happiness and love. As I descended from the platform and started forward to clasp her in my arms the entire audience seemed to vanish into nothingness, and my head began to whirl. I turned and looked backward, and to my great astonishment and confusion beheld myself still seated upon the platform. It seemed to me that I was divided into two parts. I rubbed my eyes in amazement and looked again. There was the leader of the band sitting on the platform motionless and surrounded by his faithful helpmates. I looked in the other direction. There was Arletta reclining upon the couch with her lustrous eyes fixed upon me. I glanced down at myself and found that I was the same old John Convert dressed in sailor's clothes.

For several moments I stood there buried in the depth of serious meditation. Then slowly walking over near Arletta, I stooped and resting upon one foot and knee, I tenderly took her hand in mine and bowed my head in reverence. I understood it all now.

CHAPTER XVII

"What a wonderful world this is! What writer of fiction could draw upon his imagination for anything to compare with this extraordinary freak of nature?" soliloquized I, arising and taking a seat opposite Arletta and staring at her in amazement.

"There is no such thing as a freak of nature," corrected Arletta, "the utmost reason prevails for all of her acts; but the simplest of nature's laws appears complex and incomprehensible to the Apeman, who merely uses his brain as an organ for self-gratification instead of an instrument to grasp natural laws for which purpose it is intended. And therefore, while your famous Apemen stunt the growth of the brain by misusing it for the base purpose of accumulating individual wealth, our great men utilized their brains to receive, understand and operate the wise laws established by nature for the equal benefit and betterment of all mankind. And therein lies the chief difference between the piece of human machinery your soul now occupies and that which it once directed over four thousand years ago. Behold," said she, dramatically pointing at the director of the band, "that you were," and then casting her eyes upon me, "that you are. Does your mind lack the strength to fully appreciate the magnificent lesson nature has forced upon you, and which, no doubt, stands unparalleled in the history of your species?

"Oh, if each little Apeman could only be made to understand, that the present body is but one little installment of the innumerable lives his soul has to preside over, and that the rich and powerful today may be the weak and lowly tomorrow, he would begin at once to treat all living things with equal kindness and sympathy. If he could only realize that the dog he kicks, the horse he mistreats, or the poor mental or physical weakling he takes advantage of might possibly be impelled by the same soul that moved the form of his deceased father, mother, or offspring, his selfishness and cruelty would vanish forever. If he could only comprehend that the soul suffers as well as the flesh it stimulates, and that it must naturally continue to do so, more or less, until every particle of living matter has been cleansed and remoulded into the highest type of earthly being, he would strive to reach perfection himself and urge others to do likewise. For all terrestrial life must go up or down together; a moment of selfish pleasure now, means an age of suffering and torment in the future. Such are the immutable laws of nature. And these laws must be obeyed before mankind can climb the ladder of greatness.

"It sometimes appears as if Natural Law works very slowly before reaching a given point, but there is always a reason for every one of its movements. While apparently incomprehensible, still it was in accordance with an eternal law, that you were sent back here again after an interim of over tour thousand years. My soul, which had been held a captive during all that time, might have remained here for millions of years had you not come back to release it from its peculiar bondage. But you did return, and nature thereby demonstrated that it never forgets anything, from the workings of the great living things of which the suns, moons and planets are but mere organs, down to the minutest microbe of the microbe. So you can readily perceive that at least two of the bodies which your soul has inhabited were chosen to perform great services for the human race. First, by a natural course of instruction, you proved to the Sagemen over four thousand years ago that the soul was indestructible. And now, through a mysterious operation of nature you are brought back here in an inferior organism and have had a positive manifestation of the identical principle thus established, in order that you might resurrect and make known to all mankind the unalterable truth--Natural Law. Do you not feel highly honored to be called upon twice for such grand missions?"

"But I cannot understand," said I, "why nature, after having allowed the Sagemen to reach such a state of physical, mental and moral superiority, should destroy them just when they had reached the threshold of success."

"Nature did not destroy the Sagemen," replied Arletta, "they extinguished themselves in making an effort to accomplish something beyond their powers. They tried to operate a law with which they had not become sufficiently familiar to insure success. If one of your little

Apemen experiments with steam or dynamite and is blown to atoms, that is his own fault, not nature's.

"For a thousand years the Sagemen had made remarkable progress along scientific lines. They had mastered themselves, and had learned to think both individually and collectively; and also to properly distribute and enjoy the products of their combined efforts. They had acquired a thorough knowledge of the particles of which the earth is composed, and had secured control of the atmosphere that surrounds it. They had harnessed the chemical properties of the sun after reaching the earth, and had gained possession of many other valuable utilities by following the course of Natural Law, but when they undertook to regulate the earth's path in space they simply over-stepped the confines of their abilities and failed. That was one of nature's laws they were not thoroughly acquainted with. However, as it requires many drawbacks to achieve extraordinary success in all things, humanity should not be discouraged over this failure, but gradually work its way up again until it has not only reached, but surpassed the high standard of excellence attained by the Sagemen.

"In the great stretch called time, the length of one little human existence is but a mere fraction of a moment. Therefore, one should devote his best efforts during that brief period, to making better the conditions of the place in which he has to spend many lives, for, according to what he has done in one life, so must he contend with in the next. If, while possessing physical and mental strength in one body, he assists in upholding a corrupt social system which takes from the weak and gives to the strong, he must expect these same conditions to exist when he returns as a weakling. For as long as hogs are bred and slaughtered, so must he take his chances of being one of them. How much better to help mankind seek a higher plane of intelligence, in which equality would be a reality, thus firmly cementing the tie of sympathy and love between all living things. In this case he would have no fear concerning his chances upon the next visit, no matter in what form he might appear. And how much better to carry on the work of decreasing the birth of the lower animals and increasing the numbers and quality of the higher species, until there was nothing left on earth but the very best type of human beings for all souls to inhabit.

"Natural Law is very easily understood if the mind is properly directed toward it. Great thoughts are easily conveyed from one to another after the strong intellects have conceived them. Nature itself is simply the principle of the utilization of creative life. This principle plainly shows an evolutionary tendency of all living particles toward a final state of complete intelligence. This intelligence is absorbed by the mind. The mind itself is expanded in proportion to the quantity it takes in, and is capable of directing it for either good or evil purposes. The difference between good and evil is merely that between unselfishness and selfishness. Owing to its immature growth, the mind has a tendency to use the intelligence it acquires for selfish ends. And here is where the soul or conscience has its work to perform, in trying to direct it into good channels.

"Intelligence means the ability to think, or understand the thoughts conceived by others. The most intelligent mind will listen to the soul, and use the thought as an unselfish medium with which to aid others. The poorly developed brain stifles the pleadings of the conscience and utilizes it as a selfish weapon to secure the power to take from others. The battle of existence is constantly carried on between selfishness, which is bred from the very lowest form of intelligence, and unselfishness, which represents the very highest state of mentality. A well-balanced mind wants all men to enjoy equal rights and opportunities in common with one another, affording each a chance to rise as high as his capabilities will permit. For the more intelligent beings there are in existence, the better for all concerned. If you want to eradicate disease, you must stamp out the conditions that breed it. Before you can reach the highest form of intelligence, you must exterminate the causes which create selfishness. And he who labors to improve others, unconsciously produces better conditions for himself."

CHAPTER XVIII

"The history of Sageland," continued Arletta, "during one thousand years prior to the great catastrophe was simply a record of heaven on earth, in which the inhabitants lived for and loved one another. The abolition of the pernicious system of individual accumulation was the direct cause for the existence of this beautiful state of affairs. For when the people discovered that they could no longer hoard up wealth for personal advantage, but were required to give their best efforts toward general production in exchange for the necessities of life, they lost all evil desires and endeavored to secure the highest esteem of their fellow- beings by perfecting themselves mentally, morally and physically for the good of the community.

"The system by which the State required each individual to devote a portion of his time toward general production, and which gave him in return for his services a home, food, clothes, education, entertainment, and, in fact, everything necessary to his welfare and comfort, is so simple and easy of comprehension that any living thing above the intellectual line of the Ape should be able to understand it.

"In the first place, the State was simply the people--all of the people--working harmoniously together as a unit. Every child was educated from its infancy in the economic principles of the State, and upon arriving at maturity was given a voice in its government. There were no privileges whatsoever granted to any particular person or persons, no matter how superior their intelligence nor how valuable the services they rendered to the country. As long as any one, whether strong or weak, lived up to the laws of the State and applied himself to the best of his ability, just so long was he allowed a voice in the government and an equal proportion of the benefits accorded to all. Both men and women enjoyed equal rights. Every man and woman in the country was a public servant; they all worked for the public good.

Each law adopted was put into force through the direct vote of all the people. Municipal and sectional laws were made uniform throughout the entire nation. The public officials were chosen from the wisest men and women of the land. These officials formulated the laws, but none of them became operative until sanctioned by the people through suffrage. And no matter whether the law was great or trivial, it was left for the people to decide whether they would accept or reject it. The majority always settled the question, and the law went into operation for a stated period, at the expiration of which time the question would again be reconsidered and voted upon if necessary. The laws were few and perfectly plain, and could not be evaded. Nor was there any advantage to be gained by evading them. The principle simply decreed, that all persons must devote a certain portion of their time to advancing the conditions of the country which gave them sustenance. The State allotted to the individual the employment for which it was demonstrated he was best fitted. The working hours were few, so that there was no strain upon any one, no matter what labor he had to perform. The average length of time the individual was compelled to work for the public was four hours daily, the balance of the time being at his own disposal, but usually occupied as follows: four hours study; two hours for physical exercise and recreative games; three hours to music, painting and other intellectual amusements; three hours for nourishment and eight hours for sleep. While it was not compulsory to pass one's time as stated, still it was generally taught and believed that in so doing the individual developed his greatest qualities.

"As the State provided everything the individual needed from time of birth until death, it gave him an opportunity to devote his time to higher and purer thoughts and purposes than the mere animal desires for selfish gain, and thus exterminated the cause of deception, fraud, theft and all other crimes arising therefrom.

"According to our laws the public owned and operated everything, and produced and distributed all of its own goods. And in doing this it set aside all superfluous vocations that merely wasted public power and turned these forces into other channels for the common good. For instance: as the State owned all of the land and everything that was produced, and simply gave to the individual that which he was capable of consuming, there was no need for such things as taxes.

And without taxes there was no public labor wasted by tax collectors, lawyers, treasurers, auditors, clerks, book-keepers, etc.

"Then again, the individual being able to obtain everything free of charge, money became valueless, all the evils of the financial system eliminated, and the preponderance of labor expended in upholding this unnatural system was used for productive purposes, thus doing away with such occupations as money making, money lending, banking, broking, speculating, gambling, etc.

"Without money in existence, and labor being the only purchasing power, and as every want was satisfied by the State in return for the individual's services, there was nothing left to steal, and consequently no necessity for utilizing the labor of an army of human beings as police, detectives, judges, lawyers, juries, etc.

"And as all the public necessities were produced and distributed by the most systematic, direct, and economic methods, straight from the store- houses to the consumers, there was no use for merchants, traders, jobbers, agents, salesmen, clerks, peddlers, etc.

"As each individual was compelled to give a percentage of his time toward general production, in order to be a member, in good standing, of the community, and able to enjoy all the rights that such membership accorded, there was no chance to avoid honest work and no room for such parasites as tramps, beggars and society loafers.

"So that in abolishing the stupid system of individual accumulation and substituting nature's plan of united labor and honest distribution, all useless vocations and parasitic accessories were extirpated entirely, thus transferring that tremendous leakage of human power into honest production, the beneficial results of this change being: shorter work hours, increased education, refinement, comfort, and security for everybody, and the extermination of selfishness and crime.

"United labor merely utilized the various forces of nature, to produce and distribute all the necessities of life for the general welfare of mankind, by the most intelligent, humane, and unselfish methods."

"But," said I, as Arletta paused for a moment, "was it not a very difficult matter to make all men give their best efforts to the State when there was no incentive for personal gain other than that which everybody else received, and did not those who were capable of accomplishing more work than others, complain of the benefits given those with less ability and not so industriously inclined as themselves?"

"Those same questions were asked and answered over five thousand years ago," replied Arletta, "and were subsequently proved to be fallacies. If a man's highest aim in life is to foolishly pile up worldly products for his own piggish satisfaction, then he is really on no higher plane than the swine; for the rich accumulate wealth like the hog does filth, for what, they know not. It requires far more ability to build a strong moral character and a kindly feeling for others, than it does to accumulate a mountain of produce. The Sagemen, with their splendid intellects, would gladly have worked themselves to death for the public good had not the State restricted the working hours and required each person to give proper care and attention to himself as well as to the public.

"Immediately after discarding the old system of individual accumulation, the Sagemen passed a law that all persons refusing to do their portion of work for the public should be considered insane, and put into asylums until such time as they regained their proper senses. No work, no freedom, the statute said. But even in the beginning there was very little use for these asylums, and within two generations they became obsolete for the want of inmates. The vast majority of human beings are anxious to appear in the best possible light in the eyes of their contemporaries and are swayed either forward or backward by the sentiment of others. If public opinion says to the individual: you are held equally responsible with everybody else for the general welfare and conditions of your country, and if you show a lack of self-respect by trying to evade the small portion of work necessary to pay for your keeping, then you shall be judged mentally and morally unsound, and not fit to associate with respectable people, he will not only do all that is expected of him, but will try to out-work everybody else in order to secure the highest esteem of his fellow beings.

"The system of individual accumulation as now practiced throughout the entire world is a most brutal plan of existence. It is either directly or indirectly responsible for all the crime and suffering humanity has to contend with. It causes men to forget their souls in the desperate struggle for a mere living. It saps the strength of the individual and then censures him for being weak. It robs him of the fruits of his labor and then blames him for being poor. It forces him to steal and then punishes him for being a thief. It drives him to all sorts of crime, and then condemns him for being a criminal. It encourages and gives everything to the strong and discourages by taking everything from the weak. It originated with the primitive savages, and is the most beastly and debasing system conceivable. It keeps mankind in the very lowest stage of intelligence, and in a condition of helplessness on one side and slavery on the other. It has been saturated with so many idiotic laws and so-called remedies since its inception that it now resembles a great network of legalized corruption. Laws for this and laws for that, and laws to offset other laws are enacted until the power of the human race is wasted, in either making or breaking the innumerable edicts made to uphold a weak and rotten system.

"You cannot make right by patching up wrong. A new and effective system cannot be created by changing the features of an old and putrid one. An entirely new foundation must be constructed in order to insure solidity and strength. That was the reason the Sagemen uprooted entirely the cancerous system of individual accumulation and planted in its place the scientific and mutually beneficial plan of united labor and equal distribution as decreed by Natural Law.

"The Apeman being the foremost of living particles on earth at the present time, and nature being capable, willing and generous enough to abundantly provide for all of his needs, he should immediately cast off the yoke of greed and devote his time and best efforts to a nobler work than the petty accumulation of plunder."

CHAPTER XIX

"In equal proportion to man's moral and mental strength, so should he be well-balanced physically," proceeded Arletta. "In fact, he cannot accept his greatest opportunities unless perfectly sound and healthful. The mind derives its power of conception from the body, as well as the body secures its impetus from mind, therefore, the development of the frame should at least keep pace with that of the intellect, if not exceeding it. There is nothing more delightful to behold or conceive than a perfect physical man, whose features manifest strong moral and mental attributes, as exemplified by the portraits of the Sagemen."

"Excepting a perfect woman as depicted by yourself," thought I, with uncontrollable rapture, as I feasted my eyes upon her exquisite form and lovely countenance. Taking notice of my passionate cogitation, she interjected, "Nature created the male and female, and in order to perpetuate life itself, the union thereof is necessary; therefore, the highest aim of each should be to win and hold the love and companionship of the other. To do this successfully, each must strive to reach the very highest point of physical, as well as mental and moral excellence. Our men adored women as the most sacred and beautiful objects of life; the women revered men as the grandest things extant.

"According to the philosophy of Sage--who, by the way, was the founder of our government, and the first to expound the principles of Natural Law--men belonged to the community, and not the community to man. He contended that it was just as essential to the general welfare of the public for the individual to build himself up from a healthful standpoint, and likewise make himself pleasing to the eyes of others, as it was to construct sanitary and artistic houses.

"Health and beauty are natural; disease and deformity are acquired, and are therefore crimes against mankind. There are three good reasons why it is criminal for one to neglect health. First, by going contrary to Natural Law, he unfits himself to give his best labors toward the progress of his species. Second, by breeding disease in himself, he forces it into the community. Third--the most heinous crime of all--he passes down to his offspring the ghastly inheritances resulting from his own degraded weaknesses, which, in turn, are handed down from generation to generation.

"Intemperance, such as over-eating, over-drinking, over-work, over-rest, and many other forms of over-doing things, together with worry and uncleanliness, is directly responsible for disease and deformity. All living things would be healthful, if they contained enough intelligence to live according to Natural Law.

"Besides using moderation in taking nourishment, work and pleasure, the Sageman was careful about his exercises, assiduously devoting from two to three hours each day to physical culture. He practiced all manner of games and acrobatic performances, in order to bring the body up to its best possible shape. Suppleness, agility, and gracefulness were desired in preference to brute strength. Running, jumping, swimming, and flying were considered a necessary part of every one's daily routine, from early youth until old age and death."

"Flying," exclaimed I, incredulously, "you surely do not mean to inform me that the Sagemen could fly?"

"Yes," answered Arletta, "the practice of floating in the air was begun shortly prior to the great catastrophe and many of our men and women were becoming adepts at it. You see, after the Sagemen discontinued the animal method of eating flesh and other solid substances and adopted the aeriform process of nourishment, he naturally became much lighter in proportion to his bulk, and gravitation did not hold him so tightly to the earth as formerly. Of course it took many generations of tendency in that direction before he could even acquire the rudiments of aerial propulsion. But after the dread feeling of worry and want was finally eradicated from his mind by the abolition of the individual accumulative system, he then began to apply himself carefully to physical development, and as running, jumping and acrobatic work have the best symmetrical effects upon the human form, this kind of exercise was extensively followed, and as each generation succeeded in outdoing the feats of the preceding one, the entire nation finally evolved into one of extraordinary springing propensities. What will you think, when I tell you that any of our men or women could jump over the highest building there is in the world today, or run faster than any of your steam locomotives? It seems hard for you to realize such things, but still these are facts. In these days, the Apeman devotes his time to the construction of machinery with which to carry around his decaying and almost useless frame, while the Sageman utilized the power of his own body to propel himself as nature intended.

"The gradual increase from year to year, and generation to generation, of the Sageman's ability to make high leaps, and his continual desire to remain in the air as long as possible, eventually bore evolutionary results by man learning to fly. And like swimming, so with flying, the mind plays the biggest part towards its accomplishment.

"As you appear incredulous regarding my statements, I will just give you a little illustration," said Arletta, and before I was aware of her intentions she arose, and with an almost imperceptible spring went straight up to the ceiling, and then with a graceful movement somewhat similar to a fish swimming in the water, she went half way across the room and slowly descended to the floor again. "There is no good reason why a man should not fly as well as swim," said Arletta, being seated once more. "Time and inclination work wonders, and the human race has no limit to its achievements if it only takes the right course.

"In order to obtain the best results physically, the individual must live according to the simple laws of nature. Plenty of good healthful exercise must be taken regularly and without strain. The intelligent direction of the mind must also be brought into action with all muscular efforts. Man's daily employment should be a mixture of both mental and physical labor, for all brain work strains the mind and weakens the flesh, while all bodily exertion over-taxes the frame and retards the growth of intellect. Deep breathing, an abundance of pure fresh air and plenty of sunlight are indispensable to perfect health. Daily baths are essential to keep the exterior of the body clean, while the interior must be kept in good order with a moderate supply of simple, wholesome and unadulterated foods. Nature's plain beverage, water, is all that man should imbibe. No evil thoughts must be allowed to enter the mind. Cheerfulness, self-control, kindliness and optimism are great aids in promoting health. Pessimism, worry, anger, fear and violent emotions are poison to the system. There should be nothing in life to fear. The unselfish know no fear. Those who teach it, or cause others to fear are common enemies to health and progress.

"The beastly custom of drinking intoxicating liquors, now prevalent throughout the world, is one of the very worst forms of robbing the individual of his physical strength and vitality, as well as his reason and moral character.

"The tobacco habit also; that idiotic and ridiculous performance of filling the mouth with smoke merely to blow it out again, is another dangerous obstacle thrown in the path of good health. It seems strange that the Apeman cannot open his eyes wide enough to see the danger as well as the absurdity of these silly customs which sap his strength and leave him in a state of abject weakness. What a pity he cannot exert enough will power to overcome these stupid and harmful practices.

"If you want to use your faculties when you are old, exercise them properly when you are young. Improve yourself and you make better the world."

CHAPTER XX

"Sageland, previous to the catastrophe," resumed Arletta, "was a small oblong continent surrounded by what are now known as the Indian and South Atlantic Oceans. It ran from north-east to southwest. Its extreme length was nine hundred and twenty-eight miles and its greatest width was three hundred and ninety-six miles. There were a little over thirty million inhabitants in the land.

"Unlike the different countries of the present time, there were no large cities in Sageland. The population was scattered over the entire surface of the country at intervals and was domiciled in two distinct ways, namely: the rural form of dwelling, in which a single family occupied a separate house for its own private use, and the borough settlements, whereby several thousand persons lived together under one roof.

"The great structures known as borough buildings covered about a square mile of land each, and were from fifty to eighty stories in height. They were very artistically designed, most luxuriously furnished and the sanitary arrangements absolutely perfect. They contained, besides a private room for each individual, public reception rooms, libraries, music halls, theatres, gymnasiums, baths, etc. No person was allowed more than one room for private use, but a family could have a suite of apartments in proportion to its own number. The reception rooms, music halls, theatres, libraries, gymnasiums, baths, etc., were entirely public and all persons were at liberty to come or go as they pleased. The room in which you are now seated was my own private apartment in a borough building which was occupied by seven thousand people.

"I have already explained the method whereby we received our sustenance, the different aeriform substances being piped directly from the laboratories to the consumers' personal apartments, thus obviating the necessity for dining halls and kitchens.

"There being no such agency as commerce in Sageland, through which the necessities of life were bought, sold, exchanged, or stolen, there was, of course, no need for such establishments as wholesale or retail stores, banks, etc. Neither were there any jails. Great national work- shops, laboratories, and store-houses, a national auditorium, art gallery, museum, and observatory were the only buildings erected besides the rural and borough dwellings.

"The chief industries of our people were planting, reaping, condensing and distributing dietary substances; manufacturing such things as machinery, clothing, paints, musical and scientific instruments, and building. Railroads, steamships, mail service, the telegraph and telephone had become obsolete with the Sagemen. In the first place, it was not necessary for men to travel at all in person, for by the power of mind sight they were able to see what took place at any particular place on earth, and also they were capable of communicating with each other telepathically at any distance just as easily as I am now conversing with you.

"Great centrifugal and centripetal engines, capable of transplanting any quantity of material from one place to another, were constructed for carrying purposes, while automatic transmuting machines, by which one element could be turned into another, cut down the necessity of transportation to a minimum. Machinery, directed by the human mind, and deriving its power from the sun and other forces of nature, did all of the Sageman's laborious work.

"The Sageman's discovery and partial utilization of the two great forces of nature, centrifugal and centripetal power, were the causes of his final destruction, however, for he not only used them advantageously here, but by that method actually tried to regulate the earth's course in space to suit himself. And furthermore, he not only contemplated steering his own world in whatever direction or part of the heavens he might choose, but his ultimate plans were to visit, inhabit and control the movements of all the great bodies of the universe.

"These laudable purposes, while no doubt practical, failed by being undertaken prematurely as forewarned by many of our ablest thinkers, who, unfortunately, were in the minority when the question of making the initial trial was voted upon. And by this failure the earth was rent in a fearful manner, its map considerably altered and Sageland and its people wiped out of existence entirely.

"Many millions of Apemen who inhabited the balance of the globe at that time must also have perished from the effects of the awful convulsion which no doubt shook the earth to its core. And so it was, I presume, the upset atmospheric conditions of the earth resulting from this catastrophe, forty-two hundred and thirty years ago, that is responsible for the legend by which the Apeman blames the Creator for sending a flood to destroy the inhabitants of the world, good and bad alike.

"But notwithstanding his superior intellectuality the Sageman was far from being infallible. He often made mistakes as he relentlessly struggled along in search of knowledge. Natural Law teaches that the main object of life is to absorb, concentrate and utilize intelligence. Intelligence rules the universe. The Sageman considered it his duty to first control himself, then the earth, and finally the universe. But he became impatient, and wanted to explore the heavens before he had assimilated all terrestrial life, and concentrated sufficient power to insure success. He was anxious to control new worlds before he had put his own into the best order. Had he waited until the Apeman and other living particles could have reached the same state of intelligence as himself, and then concentrated and utilized the combined mental strength of the whole to solve the great problem, no doubt he would have been more successful in his first attempt at universal navigation.

"However, he tried and failed, and by that failure thoroughly demonstrated the futility of one part of humanity trying to rush ahead of the whole, and the absolute necessity for all mankind to work unitedly and harmoniously, and go forward as a unit to accomplish the greatest results within its power."

"But," inquired I, "what law or chance was it that destroyed all of your countrymen, and still preserved you through all these ages?"

"That is the most remarkable circumstance of the whole affair," answered Arletta, as she cast a loving glance in the direction of the leader of the band, and then, reverently pointing toward him, she continued, "he was the foremost man of his day, and it was generally conceded by all of our people that he was the greatest man the earth ever produced. Like Sage, the founder of our government, he lived entirely fox others. His sole aim in life was to make better the conditions of all living things; to make hardship, sorrow, suffering or misery an impossibility on earth. In order to be of the greatest service to others, he knew that he must not only be unselfish, but also build up his body, brain and character to the very highest degree of efficiency and perfection. And he did so. He built himself up from a physical, mental, and moral standpoint, until it seemed to others that he was the personification of intelligence, love, virtue, and magnificence. While possessing the greatest brain power, still he was the most humble man in Sageland. Although a giant in physical strength, yet he was as gentle as a lamb. He was the greatest thinker of all time, but there was no room in his brain for an impure thought. Notwithstanding he was still a young man, being but fifty years of age, nevertheless he had attained distinct success and fame as a musician, composer, scientist, inventor, architect, and athlete. He endeavored to unravel all the mysteries of nature which attracted his attention. One of the many occult forces he experimented with was human magnetism. It was his belief that man could preserve himself indefinitely, either in a state of animation or suspended vitality, by the strength of his own will power. He often said that, barring accidents, he would live to be a thousand years old. In order that he might thoroughly study the subject and discover, if possible, the exact forces that caused life and death, he often used me as an example for his experiments. Many times he had caused me to lie in a trance for several months' duration without the slightest change in my appearance showing itself. While my aid was necessary to suspend animation, yet when once under the influence of the strange forces by which it was accomplished, my senses departed entirely, and I had no power to revive myself, but had to depend upon him to restore consciousness. Ten days prior to the date set for the first trial whereby man was to navigate the earth in space, I allowed him to put me under the spell of these influences, and although it seems like yesterday that it happened, still over forty-two centuries have since passed by. Uncounted billions of human beings have lived, suffered and died since that time, but the same soul which guided the magnificent being who put me into that trance, has lived through it all, and by a mysterious power, has finally returned to release my soul from its incarceration. It was a natural law which caused me to sleep peacefully through all those centuries, and likewise it was according to nature's principle that you were brought back here to awaken me.

"The seed of united labor sown by the immortal Sage, which proved so prolific in love and progress to the Sagemen, was not entirely destroyed by the great catastrophe, but lay smouldering in this tomb during the dark ages of superstition, ignorance and cruel civilization, that have since elapsed, and must now be replanted in the soil of human hearts, and its benevolent results spread throughout the earth, offering peace and good will to all living things.

"And you, who are guided by the soul of my final consort," said Arletta, as the full rays of her luminous eyes were fastened upon me, "I entreat you to go forth as a messenger of truth and justice and teach the principles of Natural Law to all of your species."

CHAPTER XXI

"But what about yourself?" inquired I of Arletta, as I met her sympathetic gaze with a look of adoration. "If you would visit the different countries of the world you could revolutionize things in a very short time, I am sure. You could explain the principles of Natural Law to the people, and teach them methods of which I know nothing. The wise and learned men of the present time would understand your explanation much better, and would give the subject far more serious consideration than if I, a poor ignorant fellow with neither education nor standing, undertook to instruct them. The whole world would stop and listen to you. The inhabitants would set you up as a goddess, and rally to your standard as mistress of the earth. Besides, the power your apparently unlimited intelligence would create, your wonderful beauty would immediately charm every mortal who once set eyes on you. Kings, emperors and potentates of all kinds would fall madly in love with you at first sight, and you would have but to command to bring them to your feet as slaves ready to do your slightest bidding. To further your own purposes you could"-but here I stopped short in my recital, shocked by a thousand little demons of jealousy entering my brain as it occurred to me that perhaps Arletta would forget me entirely if all the great persons of the earth showered honors and favors upon her. I felt intensely miserable at the very idea of such a thing.

"Do not allow silly thoughts to enter your head," said she compassionately, "I shall never leave this place. This room has been the scene of the happiest hours of my life in which my coeternal companion, incased in the flesh of a real man, plighted his everlasting love and devotion to me. And by a simple and intelligent law of nature I have been held a captive in this room through countless generations to witness the transformation and return of that faithful comrade to release my soul from captivity. And now this room shall be my mortal sepulcher.

"Although I should like, ever so much, to go forth and devote many years to teaching the Apeman the glorious principles of Natural Law as prescribed by my beloved countrymen, yet it is not within my power to do so.

"Owing to the constant change in the chemical composition of the atmosphere, and the vast difference in its present arrangement and that of four thousand two hundred years ago, it would be impossible for me to live five minutes outside of this chamber. In fact I have noticed that the supply of air, which must have been hermetically sealed within this vault at the time of the catastrophe, has been gradually escaping by way of the hole through which you forced a passageway. Hence within a very short time my life will have oozed away for the want of proper stimulus. Then again, the period in which the particles of this human frame should naturally cling together has long since expired, and should I but expose myself to the elements now existing on the exterior of this place, I should no doubt, crumble into dust and be blown away with the winds. Notwithstanding nature compels the mutability of all things, its laws however remain unchangeable, and as the time has passed and the conditions altered since I should have lived my natural life, this material of which I am now composed must soon collapse, its parts disintegrate and return to the elements from whence they came.

"But my soul shall continue to live, and the same law which brought you back here to me will also bring our souls together many times and in different forms during eternity. And as you now possess the strength, intelligence and opportunity, it is your sacred duty to go forth and teach Apemen to love one another and practice kindness toward all living things, for you know not in what shape I may return. As you would be kind to me now, so must you treat all of nature's creatures. And remember, that the soul you so ardently worship now and so reverently loved over four thousand years ago, cannot return in a perfect form if there are none such forms to inhabit, or in a good and pure being if there are no such beings extant. But, on the contrary, if in the future none but good and beautiful lives exist on earth, my soul cannot possibly occupy anything else. Thus, Natural Law plainly teaches that, as you prepare earthly conditions in one form of life, so must you tolerate them in the next. In fact, our own future safety and happiness depend upon all living things reaching a high state of perfection and equality. And now," said Arletta, arising and exhibiting considerable emotion, "having briefly instructed you in Natural Law as deeply as your limited mental capacity will permit, the time has arrived that we must part, for I feel that I am growing weak and cannot live much longer. In fact, it has been through the power of my will alone that I have been kept alive until now. So prepare yourself to go."

"Go!" ejaculated I, jumping to my feet with an awful feeling of anguish as I realized the full meaning of her words. "Me, go? Never! I shall remain here and we shall die together. I could never live without you. There would be left no object in life worth living for." And then, advancing forward, I took her shapely hand in mine, and, looking directly into her lovely eyes with much earnestness, said: "I fully understand that in comparison to the Sage-man, I am a hideous and degraded creature. And I also know that the love that filled the heal is of your contemporaries for one another was sublime, having for a few moments during that musical spell been moved by the same emotions that once impelled the exalted being of which I am the re-incarnation, but believe me when I say that my love for you now is ten thousand times stronger than it was then. I worship you. I shall die for and with you. Aye, even nature itself cannot keep me alive after you have gone. I may not be the equal of the Sageman in other ways, but I shall prove that my love for you is equally as great."

During this outburst of my thoughts, Arletta stood in a motionless attitude, holding my outstretched hand and returning my excited gaze with a look of mingled pity and sorrow. "Is it possible," said she, "that there is not one Apeman in the world today with sufficient strength of character to relinquish his own selfish desires for the good of his species? Can it be that not one Apeman exists whom nature can rely upon for the great work of uplifting humanity, who is brave enough to resist the temporary fascination of a lovable woman? And have I lived to see the reincarnated soul of the bravest and noblest man that ever breathed, bound within the flesh of a wretched coward incapable of living for any greater purpose than his own self-gratification? Am I to understand that one who is controlled by the spirit of my everlasting associate, intends betraying nature's trust by shirking the responsibilities of manhood, because he lacks the courage to live? Will there be promulgated among the records of time an account of my immortal partner having deserted his post of duty by sneaking out of the world before his allotted time? Would this being, who is blessed with physical strength and a well-balanced brain, allow himself to sink to the level of a craven suicide, because he cannot secure something beyond his reach? Does he think that nature brought him into existence for no other purpose than to feed his own petty desires? Would he deliberately die like a useless poltroon, and leave the world in its present state of savagery and wretchedness, without even attempting to be of service to humanity in the very work it requires the most?"

"Stop! Enough!" cried I. "You have wounded my feelings to the very core. I'll admit that I am weak in this instance. Very weak indeed. But this is the first time that my courage has ever been assailed by anyone, and to have you above all persons, openly insinuate that I am a coward is far worse than having inflicted upon me the cruelest tortures of the Ape-man's prospective hell. I am only an Apeman, but as I said before, I love you beyond all power of expression. You no doubt, cannot understand my puny feelings any more than I can fully comprehend your lofty ideals or the full meaning of your higher knowledge of things. The very greatest hardship for me to undergo would be to live after you have passed away. But, if by the promise of so doing I can gain your respect and one encouraging look or word of approval, I will not only rescind the text of my previous statement and live, but I swear to you in the name of the Creator of the law which governs all things, that I shall strictly follow to the letter any instructions you may wish to offer concerning my future movements, no matter what they might be. So make my task a hard one, for the courage you so unfeelingly attacked must be tested to its full limits. I am ready to obey your commands."

Having thus addressed Arletta, I straightened myself up to my full height with as much dignity as I could assume, folded my arms across my chest and awaited her orders.

"The Sagemen never urged their desires by a command," replied Arletta, "they simply requested that which they would like to have done. The request I shall make concerning your future duty can be incorporated in a very few words, but it will require a lifetime and great strength of character to execute. But as you have promised like a man to follow my instructions, I shall die with implicit confidence in your determination to do so. So consider well the following mandate, for it contains the essence which will stimulate you to heroic deeds:

"Always consult your soul for advice,

"Do no act your conscience will not sanction."

Three times Arletta slowly repeated this precept, and then placing her hands upon my shoulders, she continued: "The first time you act contrary to the admonition of your soul, then you will have broken your promise to me. Now go," said she, turning me about until I faced the doorway, "I must request your immediate departure. Go, and try to be a man. We shall meet many times in the future, so while you have the chance try and make better the conditions of life, that we may eventually meet on the same plane of equality without the shadow of strife or animosity to mar our happiness. Good-bye."

With the meaning of these words ringing in my head, I fully understood that my audience with Arletta was at an end, and overcome with grief and gloom I weakly responded, "good-bye," and then added, "I shall never break my promise." Then with a heavy tread I walked to the opening through which I had entered, turned half around and took one long, last, loving look at Arletta and passed into the corridor beyond. At the same time I fancied I heard her gently sobbing.

CHAPTER XXII

Suffering with a dejected feeling of despair, I wended my way through the chaotic anterior hall in search of the hole through which I had so miraculously entered. It seemed as if life's sole aim had suddenly been stricken from the range of my vision. I could not understand why nature should be so cruel as to give me but one momentary glimpse of that angelic mortal and then thrust me away from her in such an indifferent manner. I wondered why the world was not populated exclusively by such lovely beings. Was it because the people themselves, through their individual accumulative system, created conditions whereby only the most abject and debased mortals could survive? Was this system responsible for petty selfishness, instead of conscience governing man, causing him in his greedy scramble for temporary gain, to keep others in a state of helplessness, ignorance, and squalor, thus propagating an inferior race of physical, mental, and moral pigmies as the foremost inhabitants of the earth? Why could not humanity organize itself as a great unit of unselfish effort and equality, for the purpose of uplifting and strengthening all of its component parts, instead of those parts pulling down, weakening, and destroying one another in a ferocious struggle for individual predominance?

As these and similar thoughts crowded themselves into my brain, my attention was attracted by soft strains of music emanating from the room I had just left, and I stood still and listened. Arletta had evidently set the orchestral mechanism in motion again, and was accompanying it by tenderly singing her own requiem. With tremulous modulation, her vocal chords produced sounds such as I had never heard before, and of which I am powerless to give the faintest description. Like a statue, I stood and listened to the almost supernatural melody, and inwardly prayed that it might continue forever. But suddenly both the music and singing ended, and absolute quietness prevailed. It may have been a pure fancy on my part, but as I waited in breathless silence, hoping for more music, the apparition of Arletta seemed to pass directly over my head, and continued right on up through the solid roof of the hallway. Startled beyond expression at what I now consider a mere delusion, I shouted Arletta at the top of my voice several times, and receiving no answer, either telepathically or phonetically, I came to the awful conclusion that she was no more.

Is it unmanly to cry? If so, I must confess my unmanliness, for on this occasion it was impossible for me to repress the tears from coursing down my cheeks, as I realized that the last of nature's grandest and noblest earthly beings had passed away. But the tears I shed apparently softened my nature, and as I stood buried in the depth of meditation concerning the preceding events, I became impregnated with the desire to try and do some real good in the world; to make myself useful to mankind; to live for others instead of myself alone. And then and there I resolved that I would devote the remainder of my natural life to teaching human beings the beautiful principles of Natural Law, as I understood them, without expectation of compensation or future reward. I would go forth, as Arletta had requested, and plant the seed of real truth, justice, love, and equality in human hearts to the best of my ability, and trust in the souls of men to further aid in its universal and everlasting productiveness. I felt positive that the theory of the Sagemen was right, and that the soul just released from Arletta was even then beginning life in a different form. Would it not be criminal on my part to make no effort to better earthly conditions for her future welfare? Perhaps, conjectured I, the soul of my own mother, who died at the time of my birth, might, even at that moment, be incased in a degraded body, surrounded by want and misery, caused by the operation of that selfish, brutal and murderous system, which encourages the strong to squeeze the very light and hope from the weak, thus forcing and keeping mankind in a state of continual degradation. A system that was created in the beginning by savages, and which is upheld at the present time by savages. And the Church, that gigantic symbol of ignorance and stupidity, not only fails to protest against such a beastly system, but actually advocates its continuance.

How long I stood there, seriously thinking on this subject, and forming new and laudable resolutions for the future, I do not know;

but at last I awoke to the fact that I was still nothing more nor less than a common adventurer, held captive on an isolated projecture in the middle of the sea. This became more apparent as I faintly heard the ocean's waves dashing against the rocks on the outside of the place. So, following in the direction of the sounds, they became louder and more distinct, until finally I found myself looking up at the very hole through which I had bored my way so unceremoniously. It was night, and I could easily distinguish the stars in the outer darkness. In making a careful survey of the surroundings, I discovered that it was going to be a much more difficult task to get out than it was to get in this extraordinary grotto. The aperture was located about three feet above my head; was barely large enough to squeeze through, and there was no way by which I could climb up to it. I observed, however, that adjoining the hole there was a huge marble pillar running upward and outward in an oblique slant, and wedged in its position by several other massive stones, but with its end protruding below the rest. So, without wasting any time, I leaped up and caught hold of it with both hands, and then, adopting the tactics of a gymnast, I began slowly working my way through the hole feet foremost, like an acrobat going over a horizontal bar. This feat, which required great muscular strength, flexibility, and tenaciousness, was the very hardest physical performance I ever accomplished, for, besides being unable to get a firm grip on it, I found, to my dismay, that the great pillar I clung to was insecure in its position, and threatened to fall and crush me beneath its weight. And as inch by inch I slowly and persistently worked my way upward and outward, so inch by inch did it slowly, but surely, work its way downward. Passing my feet and legs beyond the brink of the opening, I doubled myself up in such a way that the lower half of my body rested upon a sort of a level platform, and, with head downward, I pushed my way up until I found myself kneeling upon the crust I had previously broken through, and which I subsequently decided must have been a great pane of glass, covered by the coagulated settlings of the air, which for centuries had been forming a solid coating. I remained in a kneeling position for several moments, catching my breath and regaining strength. I feared to move, lest the thin layer upon which I rested would once more give way beneath me. It appeared to waver, as did everything else around me. After a short rest, I carefully arose to a standing position, and then observed that I was located in a sort of a pit, surrounded by rocks of various shapes and sizes. As I cautiously climbed upward, each one of them appeared to tremble at my very touch, until just as I reached the topmost point the whole mass apparently gave way at once, I lost my balance and fell forward, there was a terrible crash, and after that I became dizzy and confused.

The most peculiar and disconnected sensations then passed through my mind. First I thought there was a great hole in the side of my head, which I tried to fill with small stones. Then my head became full of holes, and finally I fancied that I possessed a half dozen heads and all of them were cut and bleeding. And then apparently all of these heads were suddenly and mysteriously severed from my body, and floated away in space like a lot of toy balloons. Following that, it felt as if every bone in my body had been broken, and I was taking these bones from their places and trying to repair them. Then I imagined that I had several different bodies, and all of them were bruised and mangled. These forms increased in numbers until I could see nothing else but them, and they appeared to be struggling to extricate themselves from beneath a huge object which seemed to grow in size until it was as large as a mountain. Finally released, they began climbing up the mountain until the summit was reached and then gradually decreased until there was but one left.

"What is the matter with me?" I wondered. "Who am I, what am I, and where do I belong?" I tried to think coherently, but my mind was feeble and incapable of grasping an intelligent thought. Day and night went and came many times, but still I remained on that mountain wondering, wondering, wondering. Sometimes I would expand until I felt larger than the mountain itself; then again I would shrink to the size of a flea. One time I would feel as if I were up near the North Pole, surrounded by ice and freezing to death. At another time I would imagine that I was in the middle of the Sahara Desert, being roasted alive by the scorching rays of the sun. And, still again, I would feel that I was shipwrecked upon a barren island, and was slowly dying for the want of food and water. Sometimes I fancied that I could see ships all about me, and I would yell, and roar at the top of my voice to attract attention, but without results, as they would pass beyond view without taking any notice of me. At other times it seemed that ships would cast their anchors right in front of my eyes, and apparently remain stationed there for weeks and months at a time, and yet no one would come to my assistance. At last there appeared to be ten thousand ships all of the same pattern lowering small boats into the water, and these boats manned by stalwart oarsmen started to race with each other in my direction. What an evenly matched contest. On, on, on they came, bunched closely together, each using the same uniform stroke as if all were guided by the same coxswain. Now they were right upon me. "Great race," I shouted, as they came within hearing distance. "Hurrah! Hurrah! Hurrah!" "The poor devil is mad," I fancied I heard someone exclaim, and my mind became a blank.

CHAPTER XXIII

FIRST VOICE: "This is a most peculiar case of enteric fever, in which the patient baffles all medical aid towards a cure. The fellow has been out of his head ever since he was brought here, two months ago, and fancies that he has been in a trance since the time of Noah and the Ark. He has a strange hallucination that he can be awakened from his protracted nap by a kiss from a certain female, whom he describes as Arletta the Beautiful. Although he is as crazy as a loon, yet some of his utterances are really remarkable for the depth of logic they contain. The case has its amusing side also, for every woman by the name of Arletta who visits this hospital cannot resist the temptation of kissing the man, in order to ascertain whether they possess the secret charm to restore his right senses. But so far the osculatory experiment has proved a dire failure. He bears evidence of being a handsome and distinguished person, notwithstanding he is a charity patient, and without friends. His identification is unknown, he having been picked up on the street in his present condition by the police, who had him sent here. I fully believe-but Miss, you are crying. Evidently your nature is too emotional for the sick room, so come, we will pass along."

SECOND VOICE: "No, wait a moment, Doctor. I--I think--I am positive that I know this man. In fact, I was very well acquainted with him a few years ago. It all seems so strange, but-well-you see-he often told me that he loved me. Yes, my name is Arletta, but I did not love him, nor even like him. My father and mother hated him, and we all had to secretly leave home and travel abroad in order for me to avoid his undesirable attentions. But notwithstanding that, my heart now bleeds for him in his terrible plight, and I want to do something for him. My conscience would not allow me to pass along without trying to aid him. You say that in his ravings he claims that a kiss from Arletta would save him. I have never done such a thing before in my life, but now an irresistible force from within has taken possession of me and I feel that it is my duty to try the experiment myself, and see if it will have the effect of restoring his normal condition. Therefore, Doctor, whether this strange method proves efficacious or not, I shall rely upon your honor to keep the secret, and never mention the incident to him. If he knew of it I should die of shame. My parents would disown me for such an act."

As though awakening from a long and profound sleep the aforesaid colloquy seemed to have been impressed upon my mind, and then I opened my eyes and looked about in astonishment. The strangeness of my position and surroundings surprised me beyond expression. I was lying upon my back in a small narrow bed stationed within a large oblong room about one hundred by fifty feet in dimensions. Long rows of little white beds extended from one end of the apartment to the other, each containing the form of a human being. Most of these forms appeared to be soundly sleeping, some lay awake silently meditating, while others tossed about nervously from one position to another as if in terrible agony. An occasional howl of torture rent the air. Moving hither and thither among the different beds were women attired in white dresses and wearing little white caps on their heads. They carried in their hands, spoons, tumblers, trays, and various instruments and vessels of peculiar design.

At the front of my bed stood a man of medium height and build, with a heavy reddish mustache and pointed beard. At one side, half way between the head and foot of my bed, was the figure of a woman, apparently about twenty-one years of age. She was tall, slender, graceful, and magnificently gowned in street clothes. Her head was shapely and covered with an abundance of dark brown hair. Her physiognomy was intellectually strong, and the whole cast of her features showed extraordinary beauty. Her eyes were clear and bright, and expressed a tender and sympathetic nature. She was looking straight at me in a half-startled sort of a manner, and appeared to be backing away from the bed upon which I lay. As my eyes met her steady gaze I involuntarily exclaimed, "Arletta!" Then instantly my memory returned, and I remembered all that had taken place, as explained in the preceding chapters.

Notwithstanding, however, that my mind became clear and well-balanced, I became extremely puzzled as I looked at this beautiful woman, to note that she bore a striking resemblance to the sublime being, who had just passed away among the remnants of Sageland, and I became still further confounded when she timidly approached me and softly said: "You are John Convert, are you not?"

"Yes," answered I, "that is my name."

"And do you recognize me?" inquired she.

"I recognize in you a living demonstration and positive realization of the principle of re-incarnation, as embodied in the Sageman's theory of Natural Law," answered I, slowly and deliberately. "I recognize in you the soul of Arletta, of Sageland, my eternal companion, and a fulfilment of her prophecy that she would be born again. But while I make this declaration with the utmost positiveness, still I am at a loss to understand how such a thing could be, as the soul of that lovely being, having but just left its material body, should according to Natural Law, have attached itself to an embryo form, while you are a full-grown woman." At these words she appeared considerably amazed for a moment, but quickly recovering herself, she said with much sympathy and tenderness of feeling: "Come, now, Mr. Convert, try and think clearly and talk sensibly. Don't you recollect how, three years ago, we became acquainted in Paris; how persistently you followed me all over Europe, then crossed the Atlantic aboard the same steamer, and finally journeyed out West to my home? Don't you remember how angry Papa became, and how he threatened you with dire punishment if you did not stop annoying us?"

"No," said I emphatically, "there must be some mistake, for I have never visited Paris and I distinctly recollect having been in Japan three years ago, as I celebrated my nineteenth birthday in Tokio."

"Now that is absurd," said she, with a mingled look of pity and suppressed amusement. "Three years ago you told me that you were forty years old. Don't you recollect how you once cautioned me not to consider you an old man simply because your hair was white, and how angry you became because I called you Grandpa? Come now, think real hard."

At these words I began to seriously doubt my own identity, but after a moment of calm deliberation I replied, "No, I do not recollect any such happenings, and moreover, I am not forty years of age, but twenty-two, and neither is my hair white but black as you can plainly see. Will you please tell me where I am? My mind is a trifle confused at the strange surroundings."

"You are in the Ruff Hospital, New York," answered she. "I, myself, have been spending some time in this city, and, strangely enough, took a notion that I should like to see the different hospitals. It was purely accidental that I ran across you. The doctor says you have typhoid fever, but," she added, in an encouraging manner, "you will soon be well. So cheer up, and try to concentrate your mind, so that you can think properly."

"Ruff Hospital, New York!" ejaculated I, in astonishment. "How the deuce did I get away over here? Oh, I understand; I fell among the rocks and was hurt; then the sailors came and rescued me, and I was brought here. That seems like a few moments ago, but I presume at least a month must have elapsed since or the ship could not have reached this port. What month is this, January?"

"No, this is the month of March," replied she.

"March!" exclaimed I. "Great heavens, how the time has flown! Why, that is about three months that I have known absolutely nothing. Let's see, it was December 5th that I was thrown overboard, and it must have been December 7th that Arletta died. That's right, December 7, 1881-I shall always remember that date and keep it holy. It must be now March, 1882."

"Why, Mr. Convert, you are certainly dreaming," responded she, "this the year 1903, not 1882. But how strange that you should get so mixed in the dates-December 7, 1881, was the day I was born. That was over twenty-one years ago, instead of three months, as you fancy."

At this juncture the red-whiskered individual came forward and said: "It seems to be a hopeless case, Miss. He has talked in that same strain ever since he came here. Perhaps after his fever abates somewhat he may regain his equanimity, but to me it looks as if his mind will always be unbalanced. He has a nasty scar right over the temporal region, which portends ill for his future reason. Perhaps it would be better not to talk to him any further at present. He is awfully weak, and appears more excited than usual. You have evidently made some impression upon him, however, and if you would visit him every few days he might eventually be able to recognize you, which would have a strong tendency to set him mentally straight again."

"Very well," said she, hesitatingly, as if not anxious to go. "May I call and see him tomorrow, Doctor?"

"There are only three visiting days here each week, Miss; Sundays, Wednesdays and Fridays, between the hours of three and four P. M. But any time you call, if you will ask at the office for Doctor Savage, that is my name, I shall consider it a pleasant duty to render you any service within my power," replied he, looking at her with unsuppressed admiration, of which she apparently took no notice. Then continuing, he said, "Would you kindly give me your card that I may know your full name in case you call at other times than the regular visiting hours?"

She opened her pocket book as if to take out a card, stopped and reflected a moment, and then said, "Well, never mind my last name; just remember me as Arletta," and before I could collect my wits sufficiently to voice my agitated thoughts they passed from the room together.

CHAPTER XXIV

As I lay musing over the strange occurrences recorded in the previous chapter, and wondering whether my entire life was a reality or merely a peculiar dream, one of the white-capped nurses strode up to the side of my bed and without the slightest warning roughly pushed a little glass tube in my mouth. Not knowing whether she wanted me to swallow it or was merely trying to puncture a hole in my tongue, I put it out again and asked what she intended doing.

"Now look here," said she, in an irritated way, "I have about lost all patience with you, and unless you do as I tell you hereafter I shall have the orderly punish you again."

"But," said I, in amazement, "you have not mentioned yet what you would have me do."

"I have told you fully a hundred times to put this thermometer under your tongue and keep it there," replied she, exhibiting considerable temper, as she viciously jammed it once more into my mouth and twisted it under my tongue. "You are about the biggest chump that ever came into this hospital," continued she, grasping my wrist as though she intended breaking it and simultaneously taking my pulse and temperature.

A few moments later she jerked the thermometer from my mouth, glanced at it hurriedly and then entered a record upon a chart suspended from the head of my bed. Then calling one of the male attendants, she instructed him to fill the tub preparatory to giving me an ice bath. This attendant went to the corner of the room from whence he secured a bath tub on wheels, which he pushed over to the side of my bed. The tub was already partly filled with water, and I afterward learned that owing to the laziness and filthiness of the attendants, the same water was often used over and over again for the different typhoid patients. I observed that this attendant, who was otherwise called an orderly, was about as ignorant and degraded a specimen of humanity as a much boasted civilization could possibly breed.

He was about six feet tall, round-shouldered, knock-kneed, and weighed about two hundred pounds of flabby flesh, mostly covered by filthy garments. His head was pyramidal in shape, and covered by a mass of unkempt red hair. He had practically no forehead. His eyes were dull and bloodshot. His nose was flat and bent to one side, and his whole face was covered with pimples. His mouth was wide and beastly, and filled with tobacco. His mustache was irregular, and dyed almost to the roots by tobacco juice. His breath was odoriferous with fumes of whiskey, cigarettes, and foul stomach disorders, causing a poisonous stench to pollute the surrounding atmosphere. One could not look upon him without a feeling of sickening disgust. He was a twentieth century American civilized Christian. He was not, of course, the highest type of a civilized Christian, but nevertheless he was of a high enough order for a Christian community to breed, rear, and put in charge of its sick and unfortunate members. As he pushed the tub along he carelessly allowed it to strike the end of my bed, which gave me a shock as though I had been pierced by a thousand daggers, causing an involuntary groan to escape from my lips.

"Shut up there, you old duffer," said he, looking at me in a stupid, expressionless sort of a way, "you are not hurt yet. I'll give you something to cry about if you don't quit making such a fuss over nothing. You're the biggest baby I ever saw."

Having fixed the tub in position, put some pieces of ice into the water, and adjusted a small portable partition around my bed, which obstructed the view of the other patients, he called for the assistance of another attendant, and began preparations to put me into the tub. As they uncovered me, I glanced down at my emaciated form and was astounded at my own appearance. Nothing now remained of the once muscular and powerful frame I had always felt so proud of, but sickly looking skin and bones. Raising my arm to the level of my eyes I discovered that it was shriveled, and ghastly to behold, and it fell back to my side with a sickening thud for the want of strength to remain erect. It seemed as if a great fiery furnace was located within me and that I was fairly burning alive. Ten thousand different pains were shooting back and forth in every part of my body, but the most excruciating of all was a terrible pain in the center of my back, which caused me to think that my spinal column had been dislocated. And then as if all of the tortures of a refined civilization had suddenly been thrust upon me, as though some supernatural hellish agency was instrumental in causing me to go the full limit of human suffering, those two devilish orderlies took hold of me, one by the head and the other by the feet, and without any leverage whatever to break the strain upon my backbone, they raised and then dumped me into the tub of ice-water below. I had always considered myself invulnerable to bodily pain, and from early youth had schooled myself against outward manifestation of suffering, no matter what the circumstances might be, but on this occasion the power of resistance deserted me entirely and I gave vent to a howl, of rage like the bellowing of a maddened bull, and partly arising, endeavored to clutch the throat of the unfeeling beast at my head, but too weak to accomplish my purpose I fell back into the tub exhausted. At the same time the orderly took hold of my own throat and almost strangling me, beat my head against the tub several times cursing me under his breath in the vilest of language at the same time.

"Look out you don't kill him," cautioned the other orderly at the foot of the tub, "or we might have to go through another of those damned investigations."

Just then the doctor and nurse came within the inclosure, and inquired as to the cause of the commotion.

"This damned idiot has broken loose again, and I am teaching him how to behave himself," replied the orderly.

"Well, he certainly needs a lesson in good behavior," chimed in the nurse; "I cannot understand why he has not been sent over to the Island for more strenuous treatment long ago."

"Why don't you do as told?" inquired the be-whiskered Dr. Savage, in a harsh tone of voice, as he approached close to me, but I was too weak and exhausted to answer, and merely looked from one to the other with the utmost feeling of contempt. After censuring me sternly and advising me to behave myself in the future, the doctor strolled away as if such incidents were of trifling importance.

I was kept in that tub of ice-water, freezing, for fifteen minutes, while the nurse and orderlies lazily rubbed my arms, legs, and trunk, and poured pitcher after pitcher of ice-water over my head, in an effort to reduce the fever. It was a barbarous method of treatment, and seemed of several hours' duration, but it allayed that intense burning sensation, and put new life and vigor into me. As they were about to transfer me back to the bed again, I quietly informed the nurse that my back was in a terrible condition, and requested that the orderlies be instructed to handle me a little more carefully, and to take hold of my body instead of my head and feet when lifting me up, so that the strain would be less on the middle of my back.

"There is nothing the matter with your back," snapped she. "I have told you many times before that you only imagine your back hurts. Furthermore, we understand our business without any advice from you."

And with this rejoinder, the orderlies once more took hold of my head and heels, and after much tugging and twisting, managed to lift me up into the bed. This time the pain seemed even greater to bear than before, but, summoning all my will power, I managed to take the brutal treatment in silence, and said no more. Back upon the bed again, shivering and shaking with cold as though my bones would break, I was covered with heavy blankets, and shortly afterwards fell asleep, thoroughly exhausted, and feeling assured beyond a doubt that I had once more returned to civilization.

CHAPTER XXV

It is not my intention to give a full description of hospital life as it came under my personal observation, nor to recount the many cruel acts or cases of stupid negligence on the part of the house staff as perpetrated upon myself and other patients, during my stay in the Ruff Hospital as a ward patient, as to do the subject justice would require at least a volume in itself. Neither is it my desire to hold responsible any particular person or persons for the existence of such a barbarous state of affairs, in which degraded wretches inflict punishment upon the sick, knowing that this is but one of the logical results bred from the debasing system kept in force by a semi-intelligent class of selfish brutes, who are crafty enough to gain control of others by teaching the cruel and savage doctrine known as the "survival of the fittest." I have nothing but a feeling of compassion and sorrow for those abject creatures who mistreated me when I was sick, knowing that they, as well as those whom they mistreated, were but the victims of this pernicious system.

In the desperate struggle for a mere existence, most men and women are forced into employment for which they are entirely unfitted, and consequently take no other interest in their work than that of receiving their weekly or monthly stipend. This fact was thoroughly demonstrated to me by the action of several nurses who appeared to look upon their work as tasks to be executed mechanically, instead of duties to be performed with pleasure. Then again, others who really preferred the work were either kept away from it entirely, or else made dull, peevish and irritable by the great number of hours they were forced to be on duty each day, thus turning what should have been pleasant employment into a drudgery. And like the nurses, so were the orderlies; their daily work hours were so long and their pay so small that only the least intelligent and most stupid moral idiots could be secured to take positions that should be filled by men of the very highest intelligence, character and sympathy.

The physicians themselves I found to be inexperienced youths, generally masquerading under a set of whiskers, which some people are foolish enough to mistake for brains and ability. Coming direct from the medical colleges, they accepted these positions in order to gain some practical experience at the expense of the lives of the hospital patients.

The bricklayer, who devotes his life to the honorable work of building the edifice; the hod carrier, who gives his best services to the community in an equally honorable employment; the locomotive engineer, who safely carries from city to city a train load of human beings each day for many years, are only fit to be practiced upon by inexperienced physicians, and abused by irritable nurses and cruel orderlies, if they are finally overcome by sickness and enter a charity hospital for treatment.

For several days I lay upon my little ward cot in the Ruff Hospital, with my life hanging in the balance, and obliged to accept for succor the abuse and mistreatment of an inferior house staff. And worse still, I had to be an eye witness to cruelties imposed upon other and less fortunate sufferers than myself. I feel sure that many a poor fellow that I saw carried away upon a stretcher, a lifeless corpse, had given up all hope of recovery and died, for the want of a few cheering words and kindly sympathy from sonic one, instead of the constant abuse and brutality he was subjected to.

I fully believe that I myself must have inevitably succumbed to my pitiless treatment, had it not been for the fact that the young girl, Arletta, visited me each day for a half hour, bestowing upon me a tender sympathy, and manifesting the greatest concern for my welfare and recovery.

I was placed in a most peculiar position. I could get no information whatsoever from the doctors, nurses, or orderlies, and even Arletta said very little, and cautioned me against talking or exciting myself in any manner. I learned enough, however, to know that twenty-one years had actually elapsed since my wonderful experience with Arletta of Sageland, and felt convinced beyond a doubt that the beautiful young girl, who took such an interest in my welfare, was impelled by the same soul as my noble instructress in Natural Law. But I was intensely mystified and unable to conceive what had become of the time between the going of the one and the coming of the other Arletta.

Twenty-one years had been swallowed up as completely as if they had never been. Nearly one-half of my life had passed away, of which I could give absolutely no account. A look into the mirror was a convincing proof of this fact, for therein I saw a white-haired and premature old man, with a thin, haggard and drawn countenance, which plainly showed the results of having lived a life of hardship, and almost unrecognizable as my own face. My heavy black mustache was gone, and in its place nothing but white stubble remained. The more I endeavored to reach some tangible solution of the mystery, the more confused I became. According to the girl, Arletta's story, I had been introduced to her at a reception in Paris three years previously, had apparently fallen desperately in love with her, and made myself obnoxious by following her everywhere she went for several months. But as neither she nor her parents liked me, I was finally eluded, and had not been seen for over two years. According to her account, I was generally looked upon as a rich gentleman of leisure and bad habits, who did nothing but travel and spend money recklessly. This being the case, the foremost questions of my mind were: Where had I gotten the money to spend so extravagantly? Had I lived those twenty-one years as a rational being, earning and accumulating wealth and still not knowing anything about it? Arletta of Sageland had told me that there was no such thing as a freak of nature, and that everything worked according to Natural Law, but my case certainly seemed to be an exception to the general run of things. What would be the final outcome of my mysterious career, was a question to be answered that was entirely beyond the limits of my imagination. It gave me a severe pain in the head to contemplate beyond the surface of the subject, and I finally allowed the whole matter to slip from my attention and bent my efforts toward recovery from the effects of my physical ailments.

One day Arletta said to me in as kindly a manner as possible: "Mr. Convert, the doctor informs me that the reason you do not get well is because you lack the will power to do so."

"Will power," exclaimed I, "my dear sweet girl, that is all I have left. It is the only force that is keeping me alive in the face of the cruelest treatment man could possibly receive at the hands of his fellow beings.

Without will power I should have been killed long ago by these people, but through that agency alone I have been enabled to defy death and I promise you that I shall get well in spite of them."

"Why, Mr. Convert, how can you talk so harshly against these kind people? I am sure they are doing everything within their power to make you well."

"You think so because you know nothing of the case," answered I. "You simply visit this place for a half hour each day, at a time that everything is moving along smoothly, and merely get a surface view of matters. It is my earnest hope that you may never get a practical insight into these things by being placed in the same position as myself or these other poor fellows all around me. If all the poor unfortunates I have seen carried out of this ward, corpses, have died for want of the same kind of will power I require, then all I can say is that the doctors here should be held responsible for a great many cases of actual murder."

"Why, Mr. Convert, what do you mean by talking in this way?" inquired she.

"Just this," replied I, "these doctors are treating me for the wrong ailment. I am suffering no more from the effects of typhoid fever than you are, but still these doctors are trying to cure me of a malady which does not exist. Since recovering my memory I have observed that the many typhoid patients all around me have been bathed from five to ten times daily, while my fever rises to a point which necessitates an ice bath to reduce it but once each day, and always at the same hour, five o'clock in the afternoon. In any part of the world where malaria is prevalent these symptoms indicate nothing more nor less than chills and fever and should be cured within a day or two by a few doses of quinine. I have explained this to the doctors several times, but with a wisdom born of book learning they have contemptuously disregarded my advice and still continue to treat me for enteric fever, and then lay the blame upon me for not getting well. Do not doubt me, my dear girl, I know what I am talking about. Up to a few days ago my memory was obscured, but now I am in my right senses and fully capable of using all of my reasoning faculties to their fullest extent. Some day I shall explain many strange things to you, of which you know nothing. But now I must devote all of my thoughts and forces toward regaining my former physical strength, and likewise increase my moral and mental vigor for a future great work."

Arletta said no more at that time, but to my great surprise, the next day I was transferred from the charity ward to a paid private room in another part of the hospital. The furnishings of this room were of the most luxurious description, and the nurse informed me that it was the very best and highest priced apartment in the building. I afterwards learned that the cost of renting this room, including attendance, was one hundred dollars per week. Arletta had secured it for me. It was really remarkable how quickly the value of my life increased in the eyes of those hospital attendants, by the expenditure of a little money. From a worthless proletariat I was suddenly transformed into a man of great importance. There were two private nurses to wait on me, and they moved with the celerity of antelopes in response to my slightest bidding. They appeared to be bubbling over with kindness and attention, and seemed to anticipate my every want. The orderlies treated me as if I were the crowned ruler of the universe, while the doctors displayed an unnatural politeness that was almost amusing. I found out later that Arletta was to fee them all handsomely in case of my early recovery. My new nurses were always ready to answer questions and give me any information I wanted.

Upon arriving at my new and sumptuous quarters, one of the nurses informed me that I was to receive a personal visit from the great Doctor Know-all that day. She further informed me that he was considered to be the leading physician of America and that he never made a professional call for less than one thousand dollars. As if by appointment Arletta and this doctor arrived at almost the same moment. Several of the house physicians also followed him into the room anxious to learn what diagnosis this celebrated practitioner would make of a case which had so baffled them. He lost no time in unnecessary talk but got down to work immediately, first looking over the charts which recorded my condition since my entrance to the hospital. Then he examined me carefully, with various instruments, from the tip of my head to the sole of my foot, meanwhile asking me many questions on widely different subjects.

At last he turned to the house physicians and said: "It is my opinion that when this man first entered the hospital he was merely suffering from a simple case of malaria and not enteric fever, as you have diagnosed. Since then his kidneys have become affected, and he now suffers from both malaria and lumbago. For the fever, give him ten grains of quinine three times a day for two days and gradually diminish the quantity until the fever abates entirely. Begin to feed him after the second day. For the lumbago, give him at least two quarts of lithia water to drink each day. Now as to the man's mental calibre, I find him perfectly sane and normal. But owing to a fracture of the skull sustained by him some time in the past, the two sides of his brain have become separated, causing two distinct personalities to exist. When one side of the brain works, the other side remains dormant, and vice versa. He likewise possesses a dual memory, and is only capable of recollecting events as they happen separately and distinctly, according to the side of the brain which takes the impression. Consequently, this man may have lived a perfectly sane life during the past twenty-one years, of which he claims to have no recollection. He may at any time in the future resume either personality by some slight mental disturbance, but his two personalities will always remain as strangers to each other."

Having thus delivered himself, the doctor, who apparently was bent upon making a few more thousand dollar calls that day, hurriedly, but with great dignity, strode out of the room, closely followed by the other physicians.

After they had departed, and we were alone, Arletta pulled a chair up close to the head of my bed, and, looking steadily and earnestly into my eyes, said: "I sincerely hope, Mr. Convert, that you may never again resume your other personality."

CHAPTER XXVI

The change from a charity patient to the highest paid patient in the Ruff Hospital bore magical results, and I was soon on the road to recovery. The quinine knocked all the fever out of me within two days. The food I was given to eat after fasting two months, began to strengthen me at once and within ten days I was able to walk about the room. Arletta never failed to visit me at least once each day, and on some days, two and three times. With each visit she brought flowers, fruit, or some little delicacy, and I was not long in discovering that she was taking more than an ordinary interest in me. As the days flew by, her visits became more frequent and of longer duration, until finally it seemed as if she almost lived in my apartment. Many times she came in the morning and remained all day, taking her lunch with me in the meantime. As my health improved, and I became more vigorous in bodily strength, those same feelings of admiration and love I bore for the first Arletta took a firm hold of me until it seemed that she was a part of my very life. Ah! those were happy and heavenly days indeed. The happiness I enjoyed there, was of that kind which can only exist between two souls fore-ordained and mated to each other for all eternity. As the time went by-all too rapidly-we had much to talk about. Arletta described the many progressive strides made by science and invention during the twenty-one years in which my mind was a blank, and I told her hair-raising stories of my early travels and adventures in all parts of the world. We said very little regarding my other personality. That subject appeared distasteful, and caused her to shudder whenever it was brought up. She seemed to think that in my other character I was all that was low, mean and contemptible, while she openly avowed that my present self was noble, honorable, and manly.

There was one hitch, however, which seemed to take root and stand threateningly in the path of absolute harmony between us, and that was my belief in Natural Law. She refused to believe the story I told her of the wonderful Sagewoman of whom she was the re-incarnation, claiming that it was nothing more nor less than a fancy of my disordered brain. She also seemed greatly displeased when I informed her that it was my intention to go out into the world and teach the principles of Natural Law. It pained her to think that I should allow myself to even question the authenticity and infallibility of the Bible. Her faith was so strong and her nature so gentle that I refrained from discussing the subject in any form, after I found how much she grieved over it. So I said no more about my experience with the divine Sagewoman and my promise to follow her instructions during the remainder of my natural life, but confined my conversation to other subjects, and to the full enjoyment of her daily companionship during my period of convalescence.

Day by day my weight and strength increased, until at last the time arrived for me to quit the hospital and go into the outer world. I had made no plans as to what I should do when thrown upon my own resources, but felt confident that once well and strong I should find plenty of work to do with both my hands and brain. Arletta, who appeared to have an unlimited bank account, was generously supplying me with every comfort and luxury that money could purchase, notwithstanding my earnest protests against it. The tailor had visited me, taken my measure, and returned a fine black frock suit of clothes. The hatter had furnished a silk tile, the shoemaker, shoes, and the haberdasher all the other articles necessary to complete my wearing apparel in the most up-to-date style. The barber, the manicurists, and even the chiropodist had visited me and taken extra pains in polishing me off.

"You are the handsomest old gentleman in New York," said Arletta, girlishly, as she saw me for the first time dressed in street clothes, and all ready to take my departure. "But you do not look so old, after all," she added reflectively, "if it were not for your white hair you might pass for a man of thirty-five. My! what a great big fellow you are! Really, I am afraid that all of the women at the Waldoria will become infatuated with you at first sight," continued she, critically looking me over from head to foot.

"And what do you mean by the Waldoria?" inquired I.

"The Waldoria Hotel," answered she. "I have arranged for you to live there until you have thoroughly recuperated and regained your full strength-there, now, no more objections, or I shall become angry. At present, you are in my charge, and must do just what I tell you."

"Notwithstanding I consider the task of following your instructions a most pleasant one," replied I, "still it seems to me that I am not doing exactly right in accepting your most generous offerings, for the simple reason that I shall never be able to repay you for all you have done."

"I have been amply repaid already," said Arletta, "by the miraculous transformation of a very bad and offensive man whom I did not like, into a thoroughly good one whom I do like. So say no more about the matter, for the present at least. After you have fully recovered from the effects of the terrible ordeal through which you have just passed, then I shall consider any protests you may have to offer, but not before. I have ordered the carriage to come for you at noon, and have given instructions to have you taken to the hotel. When you arrive there, you will go to the head clerk's desk and hand him your card." Here she gave me a small package of visiting cards on which was inscribed "John Convert." "You will then ask to be shown to your apartments, which have been settled for in advance for one year, after which make yourself as comfortable as possible in the place. Do not mention your business in any way as it pertains to you and me. It will be impossible for me to see you as often as I should like, but whenever it is convenient I shall have you come and see me. I am stopping at a different hotel in another part of the city, and for reasons best known to myself, I shall continue to withhold my last name from you, as you seem to have no recollection of it whatever, and it will also be necessary for the present to meet you in some out-of-the-way place, which I will designate later. Perhaps some day you will learn who I am, and all about me, but until I am ready to furnish you with further information concerning my identity, I shall rely upon your honor as a man not to undertake, by any methods whatsoever, to discover who I am, or where I reside."

With this mysterious admonition and a tender farewell, Arletta left me in the depth of meditation as to what strange occurrence nature's storehouse might still contain for me, and a few minutes later I was notified that the carriage was in waiting.

CHAPTER XXVII

It would be almost impossible to record my impressions of the different things that came to my notice for the first time in twenty-one years, as I was driven from the hospital to the hotel.

While great progress had taken place in many lines during that time, still after having had such a realistic mental picture of the wonders of Sage-land stamped upon my mind, the new inventions, such as trolley cars, automobiles, etc., which I had never seen before, seemed crude and insignificant.

As I passed from street to street I could not fail to observe the great disorder that prevailed everywhere, in the foremost city of the world. In the first place, I was struck by the inharmonious and ragged appearance of the buildings. Here was a tall skyscraper of nice white marble thirty stories high, towering up into the clouds like a great beanpole, while on one side of it was a squatty little two-story red brick structure, and on the other side a six-story brown stone building, the whole forming a most irregular and distracting appearance to the eye. In other places, right in the heart of the city, and adjoining well-designed buildings, were vacant lots inclosed by high ugly board fences, on which were painted fantastic and ridiculous advertisements.

These defects, of course, could only be thoroughly remedied by putting into force the logical economic principle of State ownership of all land and buildings, instead of permitting the individual to do as he pleased with property made valuable by the community.

The disarrangement of the buildings, however, merely typified the incongruous and illogical disorganization of the people themselves. For instance, here was a big, strong, well-fed fashionably groomed young man, walking along the street, carrying no heavier burden than a light walking stick, while just beside him was a half-starved old woman, almost bent double under the weight of a large basket of clothes she had washed for somebody else.

Then again, here were two big, strong men, perched upon the driver's seat of a magnificent carriage, drawn by two great powerful horses, and conveying about the city for recreation a dyspeptic lap-dog, while trudging along the gutter in search of work or something to eat was a weak, ill-fed, broken-down old man, who had, no doubt, given the best years of his life to the actual labor which had increased the wealth of the community.

Along the streets everywhere were dirty young boys of tender age, who should have been at school or play, rushing madly in every direction, trying to earn a few cents by the sale of newspapers, polishing shoes, and acting as chore boys.

Little brass bands were scattered about here and there, braying forth inharmoniously, and organ grinders and street piano players were rending the air with bad music in return for a few pennies, thrown to them by passing pedestrians.

Venders of fruit, shoe-strings, collar-buttons, and other light merchandise were scattered along the sidewalks and gutters, trying to earn a living by the sale of their wares, while beggars occasionally stopped the more fortunate members of society with pathetic importunities for money to buy bread.

Cabmen and horses were wasting the public power by standing idly about waiting for engagements, or else driving aimlessly in all directions, searching for patronage.

Wagons of every description were rushing about hither and thither in a wretchedly unsystematic method of retail delivery, utilizing in many cases the labor of two men and a team of horses to carry a small package several miles distant.

Countless little retail merchants, with an incalculable force of managers, clerks, book-keepers, errand boys, etc., were fairly throwing away the public power in enormous quantities through the brainless struggle of competitive trade.

All these imperfections could be extirpated by the abolition of the money system, thought I, as the carriage came to a standstill in front of a great brown stone edifice, and the driver announced that we had reached our destination. The door of the carriage was swung open by a uniformed employee, and, alighting therefrom, I was immediately ushered into the main office of the leading institution of its kind in the World--the Waldoria Hotel.

It was quite a new sensation for me to enter this great hostelry as a guest, having spent the fore part of my life as a rough adventurer who had never known the meaning of luxury or refinement. But still, somehow or other, it always seemed natural for me to carry myself properly in whatever position I happened to be placed, and on this occasion I felt composed and at my ease as I entered and made known my identity to the head clerk.

This pompous servant showed extraordinary affability and politeness toward me, which caused me to wonder how I should have been received by him had I been a shoemaker, a carpenter, or some other honest son of toil, whose labor increases the wealth of the world, instead of a moneyed gentleman of leisure and extravagance, as he evidently supposed me to be.

"Your secretary has deposited five thousand dollars to your credit here, Mr. Convert," said he, handing me a blank cheque book, "so if you will kindly give me your signature for certification, you can then draw upon that amount as you see fit."

In astonishment I was about to inform him that I had no secretary, and that the money was not mine, when it occurred to me that perhaps Arletta, or her agent, if she had one, must have pretended to be my secretary. So I said nothing and did as requested.

Upon being shown to my apartments, a handsomely furnished suite of two rooms and a bath, upon the tenth floor, I was further amazed to find therein a trunk, two dress-suit cases, a traveling bag, and six suits of fine clothes, made in different styles, from an evening dress to a sack business suit. And the bedstead, tables and bureaus were literally covered with articles, such as a bath-robe, pajamas, underwear, shirts, collars, cuffs, gloves, hats, shoes, etc., all brand new and marked "John Convert." Upon the dressing case was a small jewel box, containing several kinds of gold cuff buttons, diamond scarf pins, and a solid gold watch, on the inside of which was inscribed, "From Arletta to John."

It took some time for me to get over the wonderment into which I was plunged at the sight of these things, and the contemplation of how far Arletta intended going before ceasing her benevolent acts towards me, but after spending an hour or two in becoming accustomed to my surroundings and putting the various articles away into the bureaus and wardrobes, I decided to make a general survey of the entire hotel premises.

I learned that the Waldoria Hotel was thirty stories high, and covered an entire block in the most fashionable district in New York City. In many ways it resembled a small city in itself, containing a bank, theatre, music hall, photograph gallery, art studio, gymnasium, laundry, electric plant, Turkish baths, tonsorial apartments, brokers' offices, library, and various ball-rooms, besides four different restaurants, two cafes, and several reception and smoking rooms for the use of its patrons.

The entire roof of the building was utilized as a promenade and summer garden for musical entertainments.

The hotel could accommodate about three thousand guests, who occupied apartments, the rentals of which cost from three to one hundred and fifty dollars per day. About two thousand employees were necessary to keep the establishment in good running order. Each floor had a separate clerk and corps of attendants, and nobody could gain admission to any of the apartment floors except the occupants and their guests.

All of the apartments of the hotel, from the magnificent "Royal Suite" to the single bedrooms of the transients, were furnished in the most luxurious manner possible. Costly draperies, priceless paintings, and exquisite furnishings of every description, adorned the drawing-rooms, ball-rooms, foyers and restaurants. Statues of ancient personages ornamented the different hallways, while the carved marble and woodwork seen everywhere showed splendid workmanship. Sweet strains of music from the orchestras stationed in different balconies could be heard in most any part of the building.

Seated on either side of the long, commodious corridors, on lounges overhung by palms and tropical plants of various descriptions, were men and women of the fashionable set, who represented the largest portion of wealth of the community.

The women with their low-cut gowns, highly perfumed, and weighted down with jewels of every kind, formed a brilliant spectacle that was bewitching and bewildering to behold. They vied with one another in the display of their gorgeous gowns and jewels, with the desire to impress upon each other thereby the wealth they possessed and the position they held in society. In fact, wealth seemed to be the predominant feature of their whole existence.

Beautiful young women scarcely out of their teens, could be seen paying all of their attentions to decrepit, bald-headed old men of apparent opulence, while on the other hand, young and athletic looking men were courting women old enough to be their grandmothers. In either case, the young were quite willing to sell their persons for wealth. These unnatural facts plainly demonstrated to what depths the human being, will go in an endeavor to secure money, or the power derived therefrom.

In the restaurants, the most criminal extravagance was practiced by these moneyed people, in many cases the costly viands and high-priced wines ordered being only partly consumed, and the remainder left to be thrown into the waste barrel. In fact, it appeared that the individual's importance was gauged by the amount of money he could spend, and men who no doubt in a great many cases squeezed the pennies from the poor laboring classes through their different financial methods of confiscation, thought nothing of spending from five to fifty dollars for a single meal.

In short, I found the Waldoria Hotel to be a sort of a heavenly place, infested principally by hellish beings-a welcome nest for people with money but a very unwelcome place for persons who had none. It made absolutely no difference how people got their money as long as they had it.

The stone masons, iron-workers, carpenters, painters, plumbers and other laborers who built the beautiful edifice were not allowed inside of it. The furniture makers, carpet and tapestry weavers, interior decorators, etc., through whose skill the hotel was made grand, were not permitted to enjoy the magnificence of their own creation. But owing to the stupid money system, which these laborers them selves help to keep in force, the results of their combined efforts were either usurped by an unproductive class fortunate enough to be born rich, or those shrewd enough to accumulate money, such as trust managers, bankers, real estate speculators, stock jobbers, and brokers, gamblers, burglars, money loan swindlers, high salaried clergymen, etc.

CHAPTER XXVIII

In looking over the daily newspapers the next morning my attention was forcefully called to the fact that fully nine-tenths of the news columns was given to the promulgation of crime in all its various forms, of which ninety per cent could be directly traced to the money evil, of which the system of individual accumulation must be held responsible. For the benefit of future generations who may desire information that will give them an exact idea of the real value of their civilized ancestors, I herewith reproduce a few extracts from the newspapers, word for word, just as the despatches were published.

"Albany, N. Y., Special Despatch: It is reported on high authority that State Senator Grab has received a half million dollars, to be distributed among the various senators and assemblymen, for the purpose of securing their votes in exchange for certain legislative laws that will favor the Gas Trust in its iniquitous squeeze of the people for higher rates. Several senators have openly threatened to vote against these measures, claiming that Senator Grab is acting the hog and will not divide the booty fairly among them."

"Fall River, Mass.: Ten thousand workingmen and women have been thrown out of employment by the mills of this city, owing to the unprecedented rise in the price of cotton, caused by the recent manipulations of that famous Wall Street speculator, Dan Bull, who by forcing up the prices in the speculative market has added millions to his own bank account during the past few weeks. The mills have been shut down indefinitely and starvation is now facing thousands of men, women and children as a consequence."

"Brooklyn, N. Y.: The marriage ceremony between the Right Reverend Q. T. Getrich, Bishop of New York, and Mrs. E. Z. Money was solemnized here today with great pomp, and attended by some of the very wealthiest and most fashionable people of the country. It has been suggested by some ungodly reprobate that perhaps the young and handsome bishop married the fat and aged widow to gain possession of her millions, but this sacrilegious imputation is furiously resented by all pious church members."

"Chicago, Ill.: Municipal ownership of public utilities seems to have been given a serious setback by the very costly and unsuccessful experiment this city undertook in operating its own electric and water plants during the past year. It appears that city officials are just as susceptible to the charm of money as private corporations, and just as willing, by corrupt methods, to fleece the public in order to obtain it. It is evident that as long as there is money in use there will always be boodlers."

"Baltimore, Md.: The pure food inspectors of this city after having made an inspection of the different canned goods, have come to the conclusion that at least ninety per cent. of the same is adulterated and that the public is being slowly poisoned to death. The greed of the various concerns which produce these things for bigger profits, causes them to use cheap chemicals in their adulterative methods in place of higher priced and genuine substances. These inspectors make the astonishing statement that they believe all foods and drinks are more or less adulterated and that in the general rush for money profits, the inhabitants of the world are actually poisoning each other by slow degrees."

"St. Louis, Mo.: An epidemic of diphtheria is raging in this city and hundreds of children are dying daily from the effects of its ravages. The deaths in most cases are children of the poorer classes who cannot afford to pay the exorbitant prices lately put upon antitoxin by the Medicine Trust. This trust, which controls the supply of antitoxin, has increased the price nearly two hundred per cent, during the past year at different intervals, until it has now become absolutely prohibitive to all except the wealthy. Unless there is something done immediately to alleviate this condition of affairs, the lives of thousands of young children will be blotted out, which might otherwise have been saved."

"Kokomo, Ind.: An awful tragedy took place in this town yesterday when Peter Doles, apparently driven insane from poverty and want of employment, killed his wife and five children by splitting their heads open with an axe, and afterward thrust a knife into his own heart.

Doles was at one time a wealthy citizen of this place, but speculation was the cause of his downfall."

"Philadelphia, Pa.: A terrible state of affairs has been brought to light here by the police who have discovered that a regular system of child murder has been in practice for some time by a syndicate of fiends who murder children for the insurance. These fiends, who secured their victims from regularly operated baby farms of illegitimate children, would have their lives insured for large sums and then destroy them afterwards, in order to obtain the insurance money."

"Paterson, N. J.: U. R. Dire was sentenced to be hung today for the murder of his father. Some time ago, young Dire obtained information that his millionaire father was about to make a new will, and cut him off without money, so he deliberately entered into a cold-blooded plan with his father's secretary to murder the old man by poison. The secretary afterward turned State's evidence and upon his testimony the young man was convicted."

"Reno, Nev.: This town was the scene of murderous outlawry last night when an organized band of burglars gained entrance to a local bank, and blew up the vaults. The night watchman discovered their presence, and raising an alarm brought the police and other citizens to the premises. Then occurred a general encounter between the police and the burglars in which over a hundred shots were fired, causing the death of three policemen, two private citizens and four of the burglars. The remainder of the desperadoes jumped on their horses and escaped with the money."

"Boston, Mass.: Rev. D. D. Sly, the eminent clergyman of this city, announced today that he has received a call from the Lord to take up his work in another field. He will leave at once for New York City, where he will take charge of a fashionable Fifth Avenue pastorate. Reverend Sly's salary will be increased from two thousand five hundred to five thousand dollars per annum through the change, which once more brings up the question as to whether the Lord was ever known to call a pastor to a new field at a lower salary."

"Buffalo, N. Y.: A case brought up in court here today shows to what extent the extortionate loan sharks will go in their greed for money. It was proved that two years ago O. U. Curr loaned Mrs. Kate Poor, a washer-woman with three small children, the sum of fifty dollars on household furniture. A contract was entered into, whereby the widow was to pay interest at the rate of twenty per cent per month until the principal had been paid. Mrs. Poor stated under oath that she has already paid Curr, in monthly installments, over three hundred dollars and that she is still indebted to him for the original loan of fifty dollars."

"Scranton, Pa.: Trades Unionism is receiving a great deal of public censure at present in this city, owing to the recent disclosure made against Judas Pilate, a union agent, who has been blackmailing different contractors for several years past, by making them pay him large sums of money, under threats of ordering union men to strike. It has been proved that Pilate has secured over fifty thousand dollars by this method. His followers, however, still remain loyal to him, notwithstanding he sold them out many times and brought disrepute upon Trades Unionism."

"Harrisburg, Pa.: The various manufacturers of cigarettes in this state have banded together to defeat the Anti-Cigarette League in its efforts to have laws passed forbidding the sale of cigarettes to children. While the manufacturers do not deny that the cigarette is wrecking the physical, mental, and moral character of the American youth, they contend that it will prove detrimental to their business interests, and thereby cause a loss of many thousand dollars if the Anti-Cigarette Law is put into effect. Reliable statistics for the past three years show that one hundred thousand children are ruined annually by smoking cigarettes."

"Pittsburg, Pa.: The Steel Trust has made a general reduction in the salaries of all its employees throughout the United States, which will decrease the wages of the worker from ten to twenty per cent, and affecting in the neighborhood of two hundred thousand men. It is estimated that this sweeping reduction will save the Steel Trust approximately twenty millions of dollars per year. Owing to the manipulations of the Wall Street schemers, this saving becomes necessary to keep the Trust in existence, as in the great merger of the several different steel companies, the actual valuation of the plants was increased one hundred times over in watered stock, so that it not only becomes necessary for those who do the labor to pay dividends on bona fide investments of the capitalists, but to pay dividends on watered stock criminally increased one hundred fold besides. This decrease in wages will cause great suffering among the laboring classes, for, owing to the increased cost of living caused by the raising of prices by the various food trusts, it is almost impossible for the ordinary man to make both ends meet. It appears to all thoughtful students of political economy that the object of those in control of the money markets is to limit the supply of necessities of life, so that the demand for them will force prices up, and, by decreasing production, will cause a superfluous quantity of labor, which, in turn, will force wages down. With cheap labor to produce, and a high selling price for the production, the trust managers and other financiers have easily solved the question of how to legally confiscate the wealth of the world."

"New York City: A great war is now being waged between the rich tenement house owners and their poor tenants on the East Side, which promises to end in lawlessness, riots, and much suffering in consequence. It appears that the owners of these houses have increased the rents from time to time until they are now beyond the reach of the tenants' ability to pay. At least three thousand of these occupants have banded together to fight the last raise, while the landlords have also combined to evict them unless they comply with the terms. The tenants, who are mostly hard working laborers, claim that it is utterly impossible for them to meet the extortionate prices of foods, fuel, gas, oil, and rents, now being forced upon them by the financiers with the small amount of wages that they receive for their work from the industrialists, and if they are evicted from their present homes it is a problem as to what they will do or where they will go. The landlords claim that is none of their concern; that they themselves are merely following the system now in existence of getting all they can, through their property rights, according to the law of supply and demand. Some of them even claim that these tenants are nothing more than vermin, anyway, and that it would be well to push them all into the East River and exterminate them entirely."

The newspaper articles, which I have reproduced, are but a few of the thousands chronicled daily of the terrible crimes which take place in all parts of civilized Christendom over the individual possession of money, or its equivalent, and they also demonstrate that after nineteen hundred years of Christianity the world still remains in a savage state. The Christian must admit, if he will stop and consider, that there must be something lacking in his religion, if after all these centuries, such barbarous conditions still exist. What is lacking? This question can be answered in a few words. The abolition of the money system. The eradication of individual accumulation. The substitution of united labor and honest distribution. The adherence to the principles of Natural Law.

Had Christ taught Natural Law instead of supernatural religion, had he been an organizer and started a movement toward the abolition of the money system and established a united labor organization in place of the system of individual accumulation, the world long ere this would have been a heavenly abiding place for the human family, instead of a seething furnace of petty quarrels, murderous fights, and selfish strife among all of the inhabitants.

Why should one hog have more to eat than another? Why should one man have more luxuries and privileges than another? Why should the man who conceives an idea receive a greater reward than he who puts the idea into execution? Why should the man who works with his brain have more of the sweets of life than he who works with his hands? Why should the man who lays the brick have more of the world's goods than he who carries the brick mortar to him? These questions do not apply alone to the capitalist, but also to the laborer as well, and as long as the laboring classes champion the cutthroat policy of grading man's allowance according to his ability, of giving more to one than another, owing to a slight difference of brain capacity, he should not, after showing his own greediness in this respect, expect the capitalist not to be greedy also. He must learn that all men should have equal opportunities and benefits from the whole production of united labor. As long as money exists, so long will fights and quarrels take place between capital and labor, and between the different branches of labor as well. The laborer will fight the capitalist until he in turn becomes a capitalist, and then he will turn about and fight the laborer. So there is but one reasonable method to pursue in order to better the conditions on earth, and to eliminate suffering and crime entirely, and that method is to strike at the very root of the cause, and abolish money and the system of individual accumulation.

CHAPTER XXIX

My sojourn at the Waldoria Hotel was a rather pleasant one in many ways. I enjoyed the luxury and refinement of the surroundings. The harmonious music of the orchestras was pleasant to listen to, and the magnificent paintings and beautiful works of art were pleasing to the eye. I also took some pleasure in wearing the different suits of fine clothes with which I had been supplied, and in making my own person appear as well as possible in the eyes of others. I even enjoyed entering the spacious and luxurious restaurants and eating sparingly of some of the delicious viands prepared by the scientific chef. In fact, the many delightful advantages to be derived from living at the Waldoria directly appealed to me as being some of the blessings supplied by nature for all human beings to enjoy.

But still there was a serious drawback to my thorough and absolute enjoyment of these conditions, when I took into consideration the fact that I was in no way responsible for their existence. I was accepting something from the community, but giving nothing in return. I felt that in living at the Waldoria, and doing no work for the community, I was like a great sponge soaking up the life-blood of honest toil, and returning nothing for the sustenance it afforded me. I felt that I should at least go to work and do something that would help to pay for my keeping. True it was that I had the money to pay for these things, but where did the money come from? Where does all money come from? To have money to pay for things does not mean that one has earned them. So I decided that I would go to work as soon as possible, and give to the community an equivalent for the things I enjoyed.

But then, the great difficulty arose when I tried to find something to do. It made little difference what kind of work I should engage in as long as it was of a productive nature. But when I went around looking for employment, I discovered that there was none to be had.

It is certainly a most unnatural system which fails to utilize all the power at its command for the good of universal production, and it seems hard to realize that such conditions can exist; but during my wanderings from street to street, store to store, and factory to factory, throughout the great commonwealth of New York, I discovered that besides myself, there were also thousands of other earnest men tramping the streets, willing, but unable, to find work. At last, however, I was put in the peculiar position of having to pay to work. One day, after a week of unsuccessful attempts to obtain employment, I ran across one of the sub-bosses of the street-cleaning department. Making known my desire to him, I was amazed when he told me that he would let me work on condition that I paid him twenty-five dollars for the job and promised to give him ten per cent. of my wages each month. He informed me that all of the men under his charge had to do likewise. In fact, he intimated that in order to hold his own position as sub-boss he had to pay this money to bosses higher up in the department.

And so in order to feel that I was at least doing something for the community to earn my right to live, I was forced to pay for the opportunity and also to aid in keeping alive one of the many systems of graft, which unnaturally swallows up the results of honest men's labor. So I began work as a street-sweeper--a position looked upon generally as one of the lowest in the scale of human employment. Why the man who sweeps the streets, making clean and wholesome the thoroughfares, which have to be traveled constantly by the people, and saving the public from filth and disease, should be looked down upon by the rest of his fellow beings for doing this great service, seems beyond the limits of sane reasoning; but such is the case in this world, where money is the god worshiped by all.

An illustrative incident occurred while I held the unique position of street-sweeper, and at the same time being a guest at the fashionable Waldoria Hotel. I had become acquainted with many of the wealthy guests of the place, who, no doubt, supposing me to be a man of riches, courted my society to some extent. In fact, I had become rather popular among the permanent residents. There was one family in particular, a certain Mrs. Snipe and her two daughters, who took every occasion to pay me attentions, until one day as I was engaged in my daily work on the street, some distance from the hotel, I noticed a carriage approaching which held Mrs. Snipe and her brood. They were all looking straight at me, but gave no sign of recognition as they passed along. That evening, after I had changed my working clothes, which by the way, resembled the white duck outfit worn by an African explorer, and, having left them in the tool-house, I went home and attired myself in evening dress. Again I met the Snipe family in one of the foyers of the hotel. The old lady, accompanied by her eligible daughters, approached me and said: "Mr. Convert, I have something awfully funny to tell you. It is just too funny to keep to myself. You have a double; we saw him today. Now, don't get angry when I tell you where we saw him and who he is, but he resembled you so much that if it were not for the position he occupied I should have sworn it was you. He was a member of the street-sweeping brigade, and if you wish to see him just go over to Fifth avenue and Twenty-sixth street tomorrow and you can see for yourself. There, now, you are not angry, are you?"

"No," answered I, "the person you refer to I have seen many times. There is nothing to be angry about. Certainly, not because he holds the honorable position of cleaning the streets which you have to travel."

"Honorable," retorted Mrs. Snipe; "you must be joking. I cannot understand how an aristocratic gentleman like yourself would otherwise make such an absurd remark."

"I am not joking at all," said I; "in my estimation, the street-sweeper belongs to the most honorable portion of mankind. He is down-trodden by society now, owing to an unnatural system which permits the strong to take the largest portion of wealth and rule; but the day will come when men who sweep the streets or occupy other positions of worth to the community, will enjoy the same luxuries and surroundings that you and other non-producers now enjoy. They will live in the palaces now occupied by the parasites who do no work. Such places as the Waldoria Hotel will be utilized for their benefit, and those who do not work, those who claim the right to live without labor, will be thrown out entirely."

"Why, Mr. Convert, what do you mean by talking in such a beastly way? If you are so fond of those vulgar street-sweepers, why don't you become one of them?"

"I have," I answered. "The man you saw today sweeping the streets was none other than myself, and I am proud of it."

"You are either joking or else you have gone out of your mind," said Mrs. Snipe with a look of disgust. But upon my reiteration that I was really the man she saw, both she and her daughters abruptly left my presence and never looked at me afterwards. They no doubt communicated the text of our conversation to the different people of the hotel, also, for I discovered later that the other guests with whom I had become acquainted, not only refused to converse with me, but regarded me as a sort of curiosity or peculiar freak of nature. They would pass me on the street, where I was working at different times, in their gorgeous carriages, and, calling each other's attention would pass jokes at my expense, and laugh loud and mockingly at me. At first these things troubled me to some degree, but gradually I gathered courage to bear their sneers-courage such as I had never experienced before.

I had faced all manner of dangers during my life without fear, but I had never known the real meaning of courage until I made up my mind to do right under all conditions, and accept the ridicule of my fellow beings without resentment. In my humble position I could now appreciate the philosophy and the true greatness of the Sagewoman's beautiful lessons of unselfishness. I felt that I was just beginning to get strong-strong in the grandest attribute a human being can possess-moral courage. The great Sagewoman's teachings on forbearance were beginning to take root in my nature. I was learning to understand that I must work and feel for others, regardless of my own selfish desires.

One day, while I was busily engaged in my daily toil, my attention became attracted to a big, fashionably dressed man, standing on the sidewalk near by, calmly smoking a high-priced cigar. He was apparently about thirty years of age, six feet tall, and weighed over two hundred pounds. He was beastly in appearance, and looked as if he considered his own selfish wants as the only things in the world worth attention. He probably had never done an honest day's labor in his life. A ragged old man, about sixty years of age, who apparently had given his whole life to productive toil, but now feeble and half-starved in appearance, approached and appealed to him for a few cents with which to buy something to eat. The big fellow roughly told him to go along and not bother him, and the old man, not doing as he was ordered, the young man deliberately swung his fist and struck the poor beggar between the eyes, knocking him senseless to the pavement. For a moment I was dumbfounded by this exhibition of brutality, and then instantly every drop of blood in my body was set boiling at the sight. I lost control of myself. My old-time pugnacious spirit asserted itself, and I sprang forward like a maddened bull, striking the brute a vicious blow upon the head with my fist, and sending him sprawling several feet away. As he scrambled to his feet, in a dazed condition, I rushed forward furiously, with the intention of felling him to the ground. After allowing him to regain his feet, I raised my arm to deal a well-directed blow with all my strength, when something within me suddenly cried out: "Don't strike." "Don't make a brute of yourself because the other did." "Let the law take its course." And, as I hesitated momentarily, there passed through my mind like an electric flash, these words:

"Always consult your soul for advice.

"Do no act your conscience will not sanction."

Then instantly recognizing the mandate I had so faithfully promised the great Sagewoman to obey, I overcame my rage and allowed my arms to fall to my sides without striking another blow.

Two policemen hurriedly approached the scene. I stated what had occurred and requested them to take the bully to jail. To my surprise, however, at the command of the well-dressed ruffian, who I afterward learned was a wealthy financier, both myself and the beggar were taken to the station-house. I was fined ten dollars, and the poor old man was sentenced to jail for thirty days.

While I knew that in this case the law of justice had been misapplied in favor of the cowardly Wretch with money, nevertheless I felt that I had gained incalculable strength in self-control by not acting contrary to the warning of my soul and making of myself the same kind of a brute as the one whom I had intended to injure.

CHAPTER XXX

Central Park is a tract of land situate in the middle of residential New York. It is oblong in shape, being two miles in length, half a mile in width and covering an area of about eight hundred and sixty acres. The ground has been artificially changed from a wild waste to one of the most beautiful spots to be found anywhere. It is coursed by a network of splendid drive-ways, equestrian roads and foot-paths running in all directions among the many little rocky hills and miniature lakes. Trees, flower-beds and shrubbery of various kinds have been cleverly arranged by skilled artists to form a delightfully picturesque effect. Chirping birds of many colors and tame squirrels in multitudinous numbers find this park a heavenly abiding place where the danger of annihilation is minimized. Playgrounds for the children are laid out in different parts of the domain while a zoological garden where animals are kept imprisoned in small cages for the term of their natural lives, is put forth as one of its many features.

As one passes through the entrance gate at Seventy-eighth street and Central Park West, and turns first to the right, then to the left, and finally to the right again, following a foot-path similar in its windings to a letter S, and crossing two small bridges, he will come to an abrupt ending of a narrow path running into an immense projecting rock. Here is located a canopied seat just large enough for two people. Facing this shelter is a small lake, on the edge of which overhanging trees afford delightful shade during the hot months. That was the place selected by Arletta for our meeting ground. It was an out-of-the-way, quiet and romantic spot where we spent many pleasant afternoons and evenings enjoying each other's company. Whenever Arletta wanted to see me she sent a note which never failed to bring me there. In fact, such a feeling of enchantment did the place hold for me, that many times I wandered out there and sat alone for hours, musing.

But notwithstanding that our many meetings had the effect of strengthening our mutual admiration and love for each other, and that I was beginning to fairly idolize this beautiful young woman, still certain things came to pass that I could not understand, and which caused me to feel that Arletta's actions were very mysterious, and that there was something about her life she was trying to withhold from me.

In the first place she would never meet me anywhere else except in that obscure nook in the park, and in departing would not permit me to escort her beyond the Seventy-eighth street entrance, where she would abruptly bid me a hasty adieu, with instructions that I must take another route.

That, in itself, appeared to be a strange proceeding, but one evening as I entered a fashionable Fifth avenue restaurant on one of my tours of inspection of plutocratic conditions, I was amazed to see her seated at one of the tables, drinking wine with a male companion. Her face was flushed from the effects of the beverage, and she was acting a trifle hilarious, and displaying traits of frivolity such as I had never observed in her before. As I caught her eye she gave a quick start, and then deliberately turned her head in another direction, and pretended not to have seen me. At this act I rushed out into the street, and it was with great difficulty that I was able to control my feelings.

The next evening I met her in the park, and was further surprised when she not only failed to mention the incident, but intimated that she had spent the evening at an entirely different place. She appeared so innocent, however, and was so charming in her manner that I almost immediately forgot the affair, and said nothing about it. A few nights later, though, as I was walking down Broadway, near Twenty-seventh street, I noticed a large crowd of men and women gathered, and questioning a bystander as to the reason thereof, I was informed that a stylishly dressed lady was "too drunk to navigate" and was in the hands of a policeman. As I craned my neck to get a glimpse of the unfortunate woman, I was shocked beyond expression to find that it was none other than Arletta who had created the commotion. Horrified, I rushed through the crowd, pushing men right and left, until I had reached the policeman, who was holding her up by the arm and trying to ascertain her name and address. She could hardly stand, and seemed dazed to the point of falling, but as I spoke her name, her memory revived somewhat, and, fixing her half-closed eyes upon me, she said: "Why, hello Jack" And then, turning to the officer, remarked: "This is my friend Jack; he will take me home." I could not understand the reason she called me Jack. She had never addressed me in that way before. But without delay I informed the policeman that I would take charge of her, and requested him to call a cab. When the vehicle arrived it became necessary for me to lift her bodily into it, and then I was at a loss to know just where to take her. In order to get away from the crowd, however, I told the driver to go on and I would give him the address later.

"Tell him to take us to the Seraglio Apartments," she mumbled.

"Do you know where the Seraglio Apartments are?" I inquired of the driver.

"Yes, sir, in Central Park West," replied he, as he whipped up his horse and started in that direction.

Arletta said no more, but remained silent, as if stupefied from the effects of the intoxicating drink she had taken.

"What a pity," thought I, as we sped along, "that this young woman, with all of her beauty, grace and charm, and with all of her splendid traits of character, should fall a victim to the awful curse of drink! Could this condition have been brought about because she had no work to perform and too much time and money to squander recklessly? What a pity that there are human beings who make and sell poisonous stuff for money which not only robs those who use it of their reasoning power, but which undermines the very foundation of the human race! Those people who make and sell liquor, knowing that it will ultimately destroy the lives of thousands of human beings, are just as much murderous poisoners as would be the chemist who would knowingly give a deadly drug to an intended suicide."

When we arrived at the apartment house, which was one of the most magnificent in New York, it was with some difficulty that I was able to arouse her sufficiently so that she could walk with my assistance. Entering the vestibule, I asked her if she could get along without further help, but she insisted that I should go to her rooms, so getting into the elevator we were taken up to the eighth floor. As though he was accustomed to this sort of an affair, the elevator attendant went ahead and opened one of the doors on the right of the hallway, and after turning on the electric light, and we had entered, he withdrew at once, quietly closing the door after him. I then found myself within one of the most elegantly furnished drawing rooms imaginable. At one end of the apartment was an archway gorgeously draped with costly tapestries which partially screened another room beyond, which served as a bed-chamber. Arletta staggered forward, half pulling me along with her into this other room, and throwing herself upon the bed, ordered me, in a dazed sort of a way, to remove her clothing. I was dumbfounded at this extraordinary command and felt that I was placed in an extremely awkward position. I did not like the idea of allowing the poor girl to remain over night, in the uncomfortable position she had taken, bound as she was by tightly fitting garments, and still I realized that it was a very delicate undertaking to follow out her instructions, knowing full well that if she were in her right senses she would be horrified at the thought of such a thing. But as I stood looking at her for several moments in a state of perplexed indecision, and wondering what course to pursue, she began to moan as if in agony, and without further hesitation I decided to go ahead and do my best to make her position more comfortable. So I began by taking off her shoes.

"What a superb foot!" mused I enthusiastically, as I unlaced and removed her pretty little shoes. "Was there ever another quite so shapely or entrancing? And the ankle! How daintily its joints showed beneath embroidered hose of exquisite material." Hardly had I begun this task before I realized that a strange magnetic force was stealing upon me. With such a feast for my eyes to contend with, it seemed as if my senses were being gradually overcome by the intoxicating clutch of voluptuous dreams.

The shoes off, I turned my attention to the collar which apparently caused her much uneasiness. The collar, as I discovered, was a part of the bodice and could not be taken off without removing the whole garment, which task required considerable time, patience, and careful maneuvering to perform. This I finally accomplished, however, with the aid of Arletta, who revived occasionally from her comatose state long enough to give a few indistinct directions, and then as my eyes rested upon her lovely arms, neck and shoulders, I was plunged into ecstatic emotion such as words have not the power to express. At last I succeeded in loosening the stays and different cords and ribbons usually worn by women, which alleviated her distress considerably, and after throwing a light robe over her form was about to, arrange her position so that she might rest comfortably, when to my utter astonishment she threw her arms around my neck, kissed me several times, and whispered in my ear, "You won't leave me alone tonight, will you, darling?"

This seemed to be almost too much for me to bear; the cravings of my sensual nature began a desperate struggle with my better self. My blood started to tingle with the heat of passion. Evil thoughts crowded themselves into my brain. The more of these evil thoughts I allowed to enter my head the less power of resistance I held against their subtle ravages. I was losing self-control. I felt powerless to battle successfully against the temptation. Stealthily walking over to the door, I softly bolted it and then stood still for some time and listened. It was past midnight and everything was quiet. I turned out the light and started to go over to Arletta. As I did so, something within me seemed to cry out with shame against such cowardice. As I paused for a moment, the voice from within became stronger in its disapproval of my intentions. Apparently I became divided into two parts, and each was struggling for the mastery of me. One side was trying with all its might to push me forward, while the other was attempting to hold me back with reproachful warnings. These two parts were my material and spiritual selves, contending for supremacy. I wavered back and forth, from one to the other, and it seemed that the material side was about to conquer and carry me down to disgrace, when suddenly there passed through my mind like a great wave of strength the Sagewoman's wonderful precept:

"Always consult your soul for advice.

"Do no act your conscience will not sanction."

And recognizing the full meaning of these words, I immediately turned about, unbolted the door, and quietly left the apartment, feeling that the soul was still master of my actions.

CHAPTER XXXI

Almost from the first day after I left the hospital I began to feel an earnest desire to follow out the instructions of the great Sage-woman in regard to teaching my fellow beings the philosophy of Natural Law, and, knowing of no better way to begin this work, I decided to go out and lecture upon the streets to all persons who might care to listen. I set aside three evenings each week to preach the Truth, and took a position at the corner of Fifth avenue, and Twenty-third street, just opposite the "Flatiron" building, with nothing but a soap-box for a platform; it was here that I devoted many evenings instructing the masses in the principles of Sagemanism. At first I felt a little awkward, and could not find sufficient words to express myself properly upon the subject, but gradually there came self-reliance, which enabled me to communicate my thoughts to others, and within a few weeks I had acquired a fluency of speech whereby I could talk for hours without embarrassment. During my first attempts at public speaking, few people would remain more than a moment or two to hear what I had to say, but with the increased force and power of speech, which I acquired with practice, my audiences grew larger and larger, until finally the streets were blockaded with their numbers at these meetings. Many of my hearers, both rich and poor alike, got into the habit of coming repeatedly to listen to these talks, and after a short time they would come to me one by one and request personal tutorage in the principles set forth. In fact, the number of these proselytes increased to such an extent, and their intentions were so earnest and serious, that it finally became necessary to engage a hall, where we might hold private meetings. It was in this way that there was finally organized the society for the propagation of the principles of Natural Law. Little by little the society gained in numerical strength, until I felt sure that the seed of this grand work had been planted in human soil for all time to come, and that its fruits would blossom forth in abundance as time passed by.

But while success appeared to be crowning my humble efforts in this direction, and the more progress I made in this propaganda, the more opposed to my methods Arletta became. She grew intensely antagonistic to my work, and tried in every way to have me discontinue it. She could not believe that all human beings were born to have equal rights and privileges in the world. She had been taught from infancy that there must always be a master and a servant, and that the Deity was responsible for the position held between them. She believed, as most good Christians do, that it is the Creator's will that some people are born in wealth and luxury, while others are born and bred in poverty and squalor. She repeatedly endeavored to persuade me to desist in the work I had undertaken and re-enter the Church as a good Christian member. My efforts to convert her as a believer in Natural Law were futile, and a great gulf seemed to be springing up and separating us from one another. I felt that I was placed in a very difficult position. On the one hand, I loved this beautiful young woman more than words can convey any idea of. She seemed to be a part of my life. I would have gladly suffered any pain or torture, if by so doing it would have afforded her one moment of pleasure. On the other hand, I had sworn most solemnly to the great Sagewoman that I would devote the remainder of my natural life to the dissemination of the principles in which she had instructed me. I often wondered at my strange predicament. Here I was being censured by the reincarnated soul of the great Sage-woman for carrying out the very work she taught me, and for fulfilling my promise to her.

The climax of this peculiar situation was reached one night at our meeting place in the park. Arletta had sent me an urgent despatch to come and see her without fail, and then she had stated that it was her intention to leave New York the next day on a protracted trip through Europe. She said she had come to bid me good-bye, and that it was to be good-bye forever, as she never intended to see me again. She appeared depressed and sad upon this occasion, and her eyes were filled with tears. In answer to my inquiry, as to her reason for leaving me in this way, she said that it was because she could not uphold me in my crusade against all recognized principles of religious beliefs.

She told me frankly that she loved me and that she cared nothing for any other man in the world except myself, but that she could not do otherwise than go away and forget me. She claimed that nothing further could come of our friendship as long as I continued an emissary of Natural Law; that her religion forbade it and her parents would oppose it; that her friends would be against it, and the whole world would sneer at it; and that to be placed in such a trying position was more than she could possibly bear. According to her, there was no good reason why I could not give up my undertaking, to please her. She had everything in the world to make me happy and was willing to give me anything within her power, if I would only relinquish my purpose and promise never to think of it again. She told me that she was wealthy, that she had millions in her own name, and that her father and uncles were multi-millionaires, to whose wealth she would be the sole heir. She said that if I would promise to quit the work I was engaged in, that she would give me her hand in marriage, and also deposit in the bank to my credit one million dollars on the following day as a dowry, with which I could do as I pleased. She was serious and, apparently in earnest, and I did not doubt one word of what she said as being the truth. So I was placed in the position of choosing between great wealth, the woman I loved, and all other earthly pleasures on the one hand, and a duty which I had solemnly sworn to perform, on the other. It was a trying situation, to say the least. With bowed head I sat and considered all phases of the matter, with much earnestness and equal indecision. To think that Arletta would leave me forever was to feel that my heart was being torn from its fastenings. To have her as my wife, this alone seemed to be the very greatest happiness that life could afford, and mayhap, the promise of a million dollars was not without its allurement. A position in the very best society of the country also loomed before my vision, as I considered these things. On the other hand, if I refused, I could look forward to a life of poverty, hard work, and the abuse of my fellow beings. The temptation was a trying one, and it seemed impossible for me to refuse Arletta's offering. As I raised my head and looked into her beautiful eyes, which expressed great love, and tenderness, and expectation, I felt that I could not say no to her. It seemed as if I had been placed between honor and temptation, and was about to fall into the arms of the latter. I hesitated a moment, undecided as to what to do, when something within me distinctly said: "Be a man. Give up all earthly pleasures during this life and teach

Natural Law, according to your promise." Then once again the wise words of the great Sagewoman passed through my mind:

"Always consult your soul for advice.

"Do no act your conscience will not sanction."

Instantly arising and feeling that I should follow the advice of my soul above all other considerations, I determined to do that which was right. I concluded that to lose Arletta, and all the pleasures incidental to a life with her, was but a temporary loss, but the opportunity of setting a great example to my fellow beings, a precedent that would have lasting influence, might never arrive again, and that it was my solemn duty to seize this chance while I had the power to do so. So, standing erect and without further hesitation, I took Arletta's hand in mine and said: "My dear girl, to lose you will cause me much suffering and pain, so much that it would be impossible for you to form any conception of it. To lose you is to deprive me of all that is dear and sweet in this life. To permit you to go without acceding to your wishes taxes my strength to the utmost limit, but believe me, the life of one little human being is of short duration in the immense sea of time, and while I am giving up the delight and pleasure of your companionship now, I am doing so in order that I may lend my feeble efforts toward the establishment of a social system whereby the conditions of this world will be made such that at some future date our souls may be able to join each other in peace and harmony and enjoy the blessings of a heavenly world, free from money, which I hope will eventually be the result of my present labors. Therefore, in acting contrary to your wishes now, I feel that I am working for your future happiness. I shall remain at my present post of duty, trying to uplift mankind, I shall follow the dictates of my conscience in doing this, and as long as the bones of my little anatomy hold together as a living being and my brain has the power to reason, I shall teach the principles of Natural Law even if all the world follows your example and turns against me."

At the conclusion of this little speech my emotion overcame me and I could say no more. Arletta also appeared overcome with sadness, and was unable to speak. She withdrew her hand from mine and without a word turned and walked slowly away, sobbing bitterly as she left. I stood and watched her retreating form in a dazed sort of a way. With each step which put us farther apart, increasing darkness obscured my vision. I wanted to call her back but a lump came in my throat and I could not speak. My brain was in a whirl. A terrible feeling of gloom over- shadowed me. I labored under great excitement. My head seemed as if it were ready to burst. I felt that I was going mad. The trees and everything else appeared to be moving about in great confusion. Those same symptoms which I experienced after falling among the rocks of Sageland returned. My body seemed to be dividing into several parts and then becoming one again. I tried to control myself but without avail. All of a sudden I saw standing before me two Arlettas, one at the right hand and the other at the left. The one at the right I instantly recognized as the great Sagewoman, while on the left stood the girl Arletta. They were facing and pointing in opposite directions. Looking to my right I saw a path running up a steep hill which seemed almost impossible to climb and upon which was inscribed the word strength. To my left I observed a path running down the hill upon which was written the word weakness. At the top of the hill everything looked bright and cheerful and orderly, while at the bottom darkness and confusion prevailed. Above the extreme top, as though stamped in space like a great rainbow, these words appeared: Natural Law, Wisdom, Love for Others. At the bottom, and almost obscured in the gloom, I faintly discerned the following: Religion, Ignorance, Love of Self.

As I stood speechless at this wonderful vision everything suddenly became dark and I knew no more.

CHAPTER XXXII

The next impression my memory has any record of was a huge ocean steamer, floating away upon the deep. Great volumes of smoke were pouring forth from its smoke-stacks as it majestically glided over the water. Upon its many decks were hundreds of human beings, scattered about in little groups, gaily chatting and enjoying to the fullest extent the delight experienced by an ocean voyage. Among all of the happy faces, however, there was one that appeared sad and forlorn. It was the face of a beautiful young woman, standing alone against the railing of the promenade deck, who was weeping in silence. As she raised her eyes and looked in my direction, I instantly recognized the girl Arletta, and realized that she was leaving me forever. And then, like one in a dream, I held out my hands and mutely implored her to return. She appeared to be within a short distance and looking straight at me, but still made no sign of recognition. I could not understand the reason for such coldness on her part, and in astonishment rubbed my eyes and looked again, when lo and behold, she had vanished from sight. But far out into the distance, almost to the horizon, I could plainly see a large steamer headed toward the vast ocean beyond. I looked around in a confused sort of a way, and discovered, to my surprise, that I was standing almost at the water's edge on one of the docks near Battery Place. It was daylight, and the sun was shining overhead. I then concluded that I must have been out of my head for some time, and questioning a stranger, who stood nearby, I learned that just fourteen hours had elapsed since I had bade Arletta good-bye, and I could form no recollection of the slightest incident that happened since then.

After watching the steamer until it had disappeared from view, I slowly walked to a bench in Battery Park and sat down, in the depths of despair, to reflect upon the strange occurrence. I must have sat there for about an hour in deep meditation, when my attention was attracted by a newspaper urchin, shouting at the top of his voice: "Paper! Extra! All about the great murder." At the same time he rushed up to me, pushed a paper into my hand, took the penny I offered him mechanically, and scampered along.

"Another murder," mused I; "what a pity human beings cannot dwell together without taking each other's lives."

Glancing over the headlines, I learned from the big black type that a beautiful young woman had been murdered in cold blood. Reading further, I was horrified to find that the young woman's name was Arletta Fogg, and that she was murdered in her own rooms, at the Seraglio Apartments, Central Park West. I could hardly believe my eyes saw the thing aright. I felt sure that it must be an optical illusion wrought by my constant thought of Arletta. I looked again and again, yet read ever the same words, and, laboring under tremendous excitement, I hurriedly perused the account of the murder. It stated that about eleven o'clock of the previous night Arletta Fogg had arrived at the apartment house, and had been taken to her rooms by the elevator attendant. A half hour later a tall, smooth-faced, white-haired gentleman arrived, and was shown to her apartments. This man was seen by the watchman to leave the place at three o'clock in the morning, and the chambermaid discovered her at ten o'clock in the morning, dead, and covered with blood from several stabs in the body.

Cold perspiration oozed from every pore of my body as I read and re-read this article, over and over again. I was puzzled, dumbfounded, horror- stricken. The description given of the apparent murderer tallied exactly with myself. Straining every nerve I endeavored to regain some impression that might lead to a knowledge of my actions from the time Arletta left me the night before until I had recovered my senses that day. But try as I might, I could no more recall to memory the slightest movement on my part during that time than I could recollect any event which happened during the twenty-one years of which my life had been a blank.

Like a man under the influence of liquor I arose and staggered hurriedly forward until I reached the "L" station where I boarded a train and rode up to Eighty-first street. Here I alighted and walked rapidly over to the Seraglio Apartments. A vast crowd of curious people was collected about the place, and as I approached, all eyes were apparently turned upon me.

Hastening forward I bounded up the entrance steps and almost flew into the vestibule. There were little knots of people standing about the hallway, talking in low tones. Even their voices hushed as I hurried into the elevator and told the attendant to take me up to the eighth floor. The operator appeared to be almost frightened out of his wits at the sight of me, but after a momentary pause he ran the elevator to the eighth floor, peering at me all the time as he might have eyed a wild beast who was about to devour him. Many people were in the upper hall- way, but looking neither to the right nor to the left, I went straight to the door of the room I had entered the night I had taken Arletta home. Finding it locked, without a moment's hesitation I threw against it, all of the force my gigantic frame could command which caused it to give way and fly open before me. I then observed that there were several men in the room, in different positions and groups, as if making a study of the surroundings. Lying upon the bed, in the room adjoining, was the form of a woman partly covered by a spread, and being examined by a man who might have been the coroner. As I rushed forward like a madman, every one there became frightened and made way for me to pass.

Approaching the bed I eagerly scanned her features, and being positive of her identity I took the inanimate form of Arletta in my arms and kissing her tenderly, was overcome by emotion.

CHAPTER XXXIII

Arrested for the murder of Arletta Fogg, after being positively identified by the elevator attendant and the night watchman as being the only person who visited her apartments on the night of the crime, was the next incident of my strange career. Thrown into prison, and caged like a savage beast in a little cell hardly large enough to turn around in, has been my lot ever since that awful tragedy. The case attracted widespread interest, and the newspapers teemed with sensational accounts of it. At the trial, all of the evidence pointed directly to me as the perpetrator of the deed. The elevator operator swore that I was the man whom he had taken to Arletta's apartments shortly after eleven o'clock that night. The watchman testified that he saw me leave her room at three o'clock in the morning. On the stand, I was made to tell, under oath, that Arletta and I had been lovers; that we had been together that same night in the park, and had parted at about half past ten o'clock; that she had informed me of her intention to never see me again. By these statements the prosecuting attorney showed the motive for the crime. I could give no account of my time between half past ten that night and the next day at noon, which was another strong point against me. I had pleaded not guilty, feeling that as I knew nothing about the crime I could not very wisely do otherwise, but also, stating that I had suffered a temporary aberration of the mind during that time, and that if I really did commit the deed, which I could not believe possible, then I had done it in an entirely different character or personality from my normal self.

My attorney endeavored to have me sham insanity during the trial, and he became irritably insolent in his manner toward me because I positively refused to do so. He told me that if I stuck to the truth I would surely be convicted, but if I followed his advice by openly assuming idiotic tactics in court and making false statements under oath, according to his directions, he could save me without any trouble. He frequently growled and cursed at me for the straightforward way that I gave my testimony, claiming that his professional reputation was being ruined by my telling the truth. He privately acknowledged that, in his opinion, I was guilty, but that if he were successful in having me acquitted, he would achieve great fame thereby, and incidentally be able to increase the size of his future clients' fees.

It was proved in court-alas, the saddest blow I had yet received, that Arletta was a frivolous young woman, who practically lived a life of ease and luxury, by monetary gifts derived from two wealthy men, one a United States Senator and the other a prominent Wall Street financier, both being high pillars of the Church, and one of them being old enough to be her grandfather. That was the most painful testimony of the whole proceedings. It did not seem possible to me that the dear, sweet, innocent girl, whom I had loved so much for her gentleness and kindness of nature, could possibly lead such a dual existence, and I could not understand why she should have deceived me, with accounts of herself so at variance with the facts. When I thought of her as she had always appeared to me, excepting those times when I saw her under the influence of liquor, she seemed like a good angel, who was far beyond even the suspicion of reproach; and so when I learned the worst, I pictured her at her best, and my love remained unshaken. While I realized that it was the poor girl's weakness that led her into temptation, still it was plain to discern that the cause of her downfall was money and the miserable creatures who utilized it to buy her very life's blood and drag her along the mire of shame. The poor girl is dead, but the great men, through whose efforts she was disgraced, are still alive, and are considered eminently respectable by both the Church and the community. The curse of money could not have been more forcibly demonstrated than by this incident. The unfortunate young woman craved money, and sold herself for it. My deepest sympathy goes after her to the grave. The finger of scorn is now raised against Arletta by the whole world, but if she could be brought back to life again, I should gladly take her by the hand and say, that my love for her was as strong as ever, and that I would defend her against the insults of the depraved society which reared and educated her in the vices which it now deplores.

It took the jury just forty-five minutes to reach a decision against me. Ten minutes of this time, as I learned from newspaper accounts, were devoted to prayer, that the Almighty should point out the right way to decide the case. Evidently the god, to whom the jury prayed, demonstrated that it was their duty to convict me. For convict me they did, by bringing in a verdict of murder in the first degree. My sentence was that I pay the penalty of the crime with my life by being electrocuted.

The trial was severe and brutal from beginning to end, from my point of view. I was bullied by the prosecutor, scathingly censured by the judge, libeled by the press, cursed by the public, and deserted by my own attorney. I was treated like a cowardly beast of the most depraved type. But with all the abuse that was heaped upon me, I endured it without a murmur, calmly claiming that I was not responsible for the deed, but perfectly willing to take any punishment the law meted out to me. There was one thing, however, which stood out prominently amidst the many shoals of my misfortune, which made me feel that I had not lived in vain. My faithful little band of followers, whom I had taught the principles of Natural Law, remained loyal to me until the very end. Not one member of the society was there who would believe that I was guilty of such an atrocious crime. They insisted that there was some mistake, and spent much time and money in trying to ferret out the mystery. They called upon me as often as the prison regulations would permit, and amid scenes that were touching, protested their undying fidelity to me and the cause I espoused. Each individual promised most solemnly to carry on the work I had begun as long as his life lasted, and I feel sure that, although the end of my time is drawing near, the work entrusted to me by the great Sagewoman is born again, and will grow to huge proportions as time passes on.

And so I have come to the end of my story. Tomorrow I must die. In writing this book, I have tried to confine myself exclusively to the truth. I have felt all along, however, my inability to do the subject justice. There are many things that the great Sagewoman tried to impress upon me which my little brain was not strong enough to grasp. There are also many things which are perfectly clear in my mind, that I have been unable to convey to others, but I have done my best, and that is all that can be expected of any one. I should like to have given more attention to the arrangement of this work, but unfortunately the time allowed me has been very short, and I have had to rush it along in order to complete it. I have produced this treatise while confined within my cell in the death-house, and therefore have had many disadvantages to contend with. I shall give the manuscript to the little body of men and women who are banded together and known as the Natural Law Society, of which I had the honor to be the founder, with the understanding that it will be published and distributed at the earliest possible date. I could wish that the reader might peruse the contents of this work a second time, if it is not asking too much; at least that he might go over carefully and thoughtfully that portion of it which contains the teachings of the great Sagewoman. While I probably have failed to present clearly much of the great wisdom directly received from her magnificent brain, there may arise in the future, wise men, who will be capable of reading in these lines much more than even I, who write them, am able to comprehend. It is my one hope that great men will spring up in the future and take hold of this work--men with minds so strong, so broad, so courageous, and so unselfish, that they will be willing to devote their lives to the noble task of trying to put the whole human race on a footing of equality. There can be no equality so long as those who are strong want to take more of nature's gifts than those who are weak, and no man can ever be great who thinks that one human being is entitled to more than another. That is selfishness. Selfishness and greatness are the extreme opposites.

This is my last day on earth, to use a common but erroneous expression. At noon today my soul will be separated from its body by the hand of man, acting according to a most unnatural, diabolical, and murderous law. And the poor unfortunate creature, who actually slays me, will do so, not because he has a thirst for blood, but for money. Money furnished by the State--a Christian civilization which bred and reared us both.

I am now forty-four years old, and have just reached the threshold of mental strength. As I am in perfect condition physically, and have a splendid constitution as a foundation, there is no good reason why I could not have lived at least forty years more. Forty years longer could I have served the world at my very best, but my fellow beings have decided to kill me, right at a time when I could have been of the most use to them. I am really sorry that I must die, not because I fear death, but because my opportunity to do good to others is taken from me. Twenty-two years ago I was anxious to die, aye even by my own hand. I thought that there was nothing to live for at that time. But the beautiful teachings of the great Sagewoman awakened new ideas of responsibility within me, and now I can see that the grandest thing within the reach of a human being is to live; live as long as nature will allow; live for others.

Natural Law teaches that it is idiotic to pray, and I believe that prayer is a form of insanity, but were I to pray, which I profess I have no idea of doing, my one request of the Creator would be that I might live out my life, in order to spread the principles of Natural Law to the furthermost corners of the earth; or, that I might be born again in a well-constructed body, with a mind capable of grasping nature's ideas in their entirety, and interpreting them to my fellow men in a way that could not be misunderstood. If the Creator would grant me this request, and I could have the ability and the power to change the conditions of the earth to those existing in Sageland before the Catastrophe, I would gladly give in exchange for the privilege, my eternal soul as a sacrifice, and take upon myself everlastingly, all of the misery, suffering, and torture now inflicted upon the rest of mankind.

Good-bye, dear reader, and may your soul always guide you.

END OF JOHN CONVERT'S WORK.

Epilogue on following pages.

EPILOGUE

FROM THE NEW YORK DAILY (Special Despatch:)

"SING SING, N. Y., 11 A. M.-Electrocution day here always attracts many curious people about the prison walls, but the much heralded execution of John Convert seems to have brought an unusual number of persons to this neighborhood, and the hill overlooking the prison is almost black with people, who have come from all parts of the State.

"Viewed from this hill, Sing Sing prison presents the appearance of a huge, square pen, covering many acres of land, and enclosed by a high, brick wall on the three land sides, and a tall, iron picket fence on the side adjoining the Hudson River.

"On the top of these walls, sentinels are stationed at intervals, who walk back and forth, armed with breech-loading rifles, and under orders to shoot dead any prisoner attempting to escape.

"Within the enclosure, at the north end, are several red brick buildings, which are used as workshops for the twelve hundred time prisoners, now incarcerated here. Running along its eastern border is a massive stone structure, about seven hundred feet long, fifty feet wide, and sixty feet high, with windows crated by heavy, iron bars. This is the main building of the prison, and is used principally as a dormitory for the inmates and offices for those who have charge of the institution.

"The extreme south end of the main building is walled off separately, and occupied exclusively by prisoners whom the State has doomed to death. This place is called the Death Chamber. Inside of this chamber is a high steel cage, four tiers high, and divided into several cells, which are about eight by six feet in dimension. Thick, cement walls, floor, and ceiling, make each cell separate and distinct from the others. Heavy doors of barred steel open outward onto the different platforms, which run all the way around the inside of the cage. Armed patrolmen, known as death guards, are kept constantly walking around these platforms. Within this cage is John Convert and many other notorious murderers, waiting their turns to be put to death as punishment for their heinous crimes.

"At the south end of the Death Chamber is a solid iron door, which leads into an adjoining little red brick building, about fifty by twenty feet in dimension, one story high, and containing two rooms. These rooms are perfectly bare, excepting that in one of them there is a chair, and in the other a table. About ten feet from the door leading from the Death Chamber is the electric chair, by which the State kills its worst criminals. In appearance it is similar to a plain, old-fashioned garden arm-chair, with a high back. Connected to this chair are several straps, by which the condemned man is harnessed in a sitting position, so that he cannot move. These straps are adjusted across the head, chest, abdomen, both fore and upper arms and the ankles. They are not bound too tightly, but left taut in order to allow for the expansion of the body. The electro connections are at the head and the inside of the right calf, the trousers being cut from the knee downward, so that a contact can be made with the bare flesh. Just back of the chair is a large closet, which conceals all of the electrical apparatus necessary to throw on or off the current at the will of the Electrician, by whose hand the condemned man is sent to eternity. Stationed within the closet, the Electrocutioner can see what is going on outside, but cannot be seen from without. Just back of the closet is a partition dividing the two rooms, through which is a door leading into it. In the center of this other room is a stationary table, upon which the autopsy is performed.

"All of the machinery has been thoroughly tested, and found to be in good running order, and neither the State's Electrician nor the Warden expect the slightest hitch in connection with today's proceedings. The twelve witnesses invited by the Warden, and made necessary by law, together with the brain experts, have arrived upon the scene, and everything is in complete readiness for the electrocution of John Convert."

FROM THE NEW YORK DAILY

(Special Despatch:)

"SING SING, N. Y., 1:15 P. M.-One of the strangest and most pathetic tragedies that has ever happened in the State of New York has just taken place within the house of electrocution here, the result of which must cause the whole civilized world to pause and shudder. Your correspondent earnestly prays that he may never again be called upon to witness another such horror, the effects of which have completely unnerved him and beggars even a faint description.

"At precisely twelve o'clock today, with the State Electrician, medical experts, and witnesses, mutely stationed in their places, the great iron door leading from the Death Chamber was suddenly swung open, and between two guards the gigantic form of John Convert walked over to the electric chair, with a firm and unfaltering step. Immediately, all eyes were turned upon him, and at the same instant there was a subdued murmur of surprise by many of those present at the magnificent appearance of the man.

"Tall and erect, with finely formed limbs, and powerfully built shoulders, he easily towered above all of the other occupants of the room. With a clean shaven face, the handsome features of which expressed extraordinary intelligence, kindness, and gentleness of nature, combined with wonderful strength of character, and a shapely head, overhung by an abundance of beautiful snow-white hair, he looked more like an ambassador from heaven than a convicted murderer. He wore a black Prince Albert suit of clothes. As he reached the side of the chair he paused, and calmly looking from one to the other of the assemblage, he began to address them in a clear and melodious voice. Almost from the first utterance, his hearers became electrified by his charming manner and eloquence, and for nearly half an hour were held spellbound, while he explained the principles of Natural Law, and the vast benefits the human race could derive by putting them into effect.

"In a convincing way he drew a beautiful picture upon the minds of those present of a heaven that should be established here on earth by and for all living things, in which they should work united and harmoniously together for a common and unselfish cause, instead of each one pulling in a different direction for his own selfish purposes. He explained that all living things were composed of the same material, which was constantly undergoing a change from life to death and from death to life by being molded and remolded into different forms, which are constructed according to the intelligence absorbed by the whole. That it is within the power of the human race, if working together as a unit, to reconstruct all living matter on earth into more perfect organisms, just as it is within the power of man to re-mould a pile of dead scrap iron into new and useful machinery. That these results could only be accomplished by the eradication of selfishness from the human race, and that it was impossible to extinguish selfishness as long as the money system was kept in force, and individuals were recompensed according to their craftiness to help themselves. He told of the soul being everlasting, and how a wise law of nature breaks the monotony of its existence through the process of re-incarnation, and that the soul of the rich aristocrat of today may be the soul of the suckling pig tomorrow. He said that it was within the power of every living thing to do good, if only following the advice of the soul, and that the oftener this advice was taken the easier it became to do right, but that the less the soul's warning was heeded, the more hardened and vile became the nature of the individual. He told of how children inherit the weaknesses of their parents, and mentioned how much grander it is for parents to give their children character without gold, than to give them gold without character.

"So earnestly and pathetically did he present the whole subject, that at the conclusion of his discourse there was not a dry eye in the room, and as he calmly took his seat in the electric chair, the whole assemblage, including the guards, stood motionless for several moments as if in a hypnotic trance. And then, as the guards reluctantly began to adjust the straps about his body, three men burst into loud sobs and rushed from the room, bitterly denouncing the electrocution as savagery, and refusing to witness the proceedings any further. With the exception of the condemned man, everybody was completely unstrung. But John Convert, in the shadow of death, did not lose his wonderful self-control for a moment, but sat with perfect equipoise in that murderous chair, calmly watching with apparent interest the work of fastening him in. "'You have that strap around the abdomen twisted,' he coolly remarked to one of the excited guards, and then quietly added, 'you are not sufficiently hardened for this kind of work, my man, but perhaps your children may be.' And as if stung by remorse at these words, the guard suddenly burst into a frenzy of grief and cried out in piteous tones: 'No, no! Don't say that! I love my children. I undertook this objectionable work for their sakes, that I might be able to give them the same advantages that other children enjoy. But now that you have spoken, I can see that I am paying for their advantages at the expense of their moral characters, and that they too might follow in my miserable footsteps and, eventually sell themselves for money. But listen, I have but just taken this position, and now I am getting my first experience at this kind of work, and I feel as if _I_ were about to commit murder. And now, after hearing your wonderful words, my conscience is crying out within me to stop, and so, in the presence of these witnesses, I not only renounce all further connection with this abominable act, but I most solemnly swear that I believe in Natural Law, and that I shall henceforth devote my life to teaching its principles to my own children, and also to those of my fellow beings. My eyes have suddenly been opened. For the first time in my life I feel like a man.'

"At this unexpected turn of affairs, the countenance of John Convert lighted up with a look of divine happiness that was truly glorious to behold, and, addressing the guard, he said: 'Well spoken, my noble man. May you accumulate sufficient strength to enable you to faithfully follow out your splendid resolution; may your future deeds be so unselfish, heroic, and fruitful, towards uplifting mankind, that the grandchildren of your enemies may live to praise your name.'

"These words seemed to have a cheering effect upon the guard, who affectionately shook the hand of Convert, and then left the room.

"During this time, however, the other guard had continued the work of adjusting the straps, and finally having them properly arranged, stepped backward a few feet and raised his left arm as a sign to the Electrocutioner in the closet that everything was in readiness. And then, just as John Convert uttered the words, 'Always Consult Your Soul for Advice,' a terrible, dull, buzzing sound took the place of his voice, his body suddenly expanded, as if about to burst, his limbs were drawn up and distorted, blue flames shot forth with a weird glow, a sickening odor of burning flesh saturated the air, and quicker than it takes to tell, the deadly current had penetrated through every fiber of his body.

"And then, as all turned away their heads from the awful sight, a loud crash was heard, and the door leading from the court-yard into the other room burst open, and in rushed the Warden, yelling like a madman: 'Stop it! For God's sake, stop it! You are killing the wrong man!' And pulling open the door of the closet which concealed the

Electrician, he threw off the current with his own hands. At the same time, amidst great confusion, several of the spectators rushed forward and began unfastening the straps which bound the unfortunate man to the chair, after which the body was carried into the other room and laid upon the table.

"Following in the footsteps of the Warden, was a tall, beautiful, young woman, hatless, and with hair disheveled and dress disarranged. She was panting heavily, and a wild, terrified look gleamed in her eyes. She appeared dazed and almost exhausted. Catching sight of Convert, she frantically tried to get near him, but was held in check by one of the doctors, while the other one made a hurried examination of the body. And then, this doctor, apparently suffering from great mental excitement, turned toward those present, and, with his eyes full of tears, chokingly whispered, 'Too late, he is dead.'

"At these terrible words, the young woman uttered a heart-piercing shriek, and, rushing forward, threw herself upon the corpse, as she piteously moaned: 'You have murdered him. You have murdered him.'"

FROM THE NEW YORK DAILY.

"The following statement, made by one of Chicago's most beautiful and brilliant young society women, is the sequel to the most extraordinary case that ever attracted public attention in this country:

"'My name is Arletta Wright. My father is R. U. Wright, of Chicago, Ill., the well-known financier and multi-millionaire. A few years ago, while in Paris, I was introduced to a man by the name of John Convert. I supposed he was an American, but at that time did not take enough interest in him to inquire as to who he was or where he came from. Later, however, I found that he was continually crossing my path, and appeared anxious to court my attention. He was a tall, well-built, handsome man, with a clean-shaven face and snow-white hair, apparently about forty years old. But there was something about his looks and actions that I did not like, and I tried to avoid him as much as possible. But he was not to be avoided very easily, and, after persistently following me all over Europe, he crossed the ocean in the same steamer, and finally came to my home in Chicago. He got to be such a nuisance that he was refused admittance to our house, and in order to get rid of him entirely, I secretly left Chicago and went abroad again. A few months afterward I returned home, and found that he had left for parts unknown, and the incident was soon forgotten.

"'During the month of March, 1903, about two and a half years later, important business called my father to New York for a stay of several months, and mother and I, accompanying him, we took apartments at the Opulent Hotel, on Broadway, near Seventy-eighth street.

"'About that time I decided to visit the different institutions of New York, and one day as I was being shown through a charity ward of the Ruff Hospital, I was astonished to see John Convert lying sick upon one of the cots. He had a wild and peculiar stare in his eyes and at first gave no sign of recognition, but seemed to be undergoing an intense" mental strain, as if trying to recall to mind some event that had escaped his memory. The doctor informed me that he was an unidentified charity patient suffering with typhoid fever and was evidently insane. He told me that the man imagined he had been in a trance for over four thousand years, and could only be brought out of it by a kiss from one he called Arletta. My heart seemed to melt with pity and sorrow, and my dislike changed into love for the man upon hearing these words, and without hesitation I kissed him, at the same time hoping most sincerely that the act would have a salutary effect. Strange as it may seem, the whole expression of his countenance changed instantly as if by some magic force; his eyes lighted up radiantly, and looking at me in great astonishment he uttered my name-Arletta. But while I was quite elated over my strange success, I was also much surprised and puzzled at his following utterances, whereby he claimed that I was the re-incarnated soul of Arletta of Sageland, who, according to his story, had died on the same day I was born, over twenty-one years before, and from which time he could form no recollection of events whatever.

"'Subsequently, I was informed by an eminent brain specialist, who examined him, that he was mentally sound, but that owing to a severe fracture of the skull received some time previously his brain had become divided into two distinct parts, causing two personalities to exist and enabling him to recollect events only as they were separately recorded on either side of the brain. By this explanation I readily understood the reason why he did not recognize me and also for the wonderful change which took place, both in his character and my feelings toward him. On that day my first and last love for man was born.

"'As time passed by, and he recovered his health and strength, he appeared to me the most beautiful character I had ever known, and with each succeeding day my love for him grew stronger. But while love formed a strong mutual link of attachment between us, another force succeeded in putting us apart.

"'He believed in Natural Law and unselfishness, with equal rights for both strong and weak alike. I believed in religion and selfishness, with the strong enjoying more earthly blessings than the weak.

"'He believed in a Supreme Being, who created immutable laws whereby the entire machinery of the universe is governed, and that these laws could no more be changed by the silly prayers of man than by the prayers of a microbe. I believed in a god to whom I could pray to change earthly conditions to suit my fancies; a god willing to grant me favors even at the expense of others.

"'He believed in re-incarnation, and the power of the soul to eventually master the flesh and create a heaven on earth. I believed in the transmigration of the soul to some obscure heaven where there would be nothing farther to do but rest during all eternity.

"'He was broad in his views and never tried to restrain me from thinking as I liked. I was narrow in mine, and quite unwilling that he should believe in any theory except my own.

"'These and other differences of opinion caused us to separate.

"'One night last June, the same night that awful murder took place in the Seraglio Apartments, I met John Convert at our regular meeting place in Central Park for the last time. It was my habit to meet him in an out-of-the-way corner of the park, because I did not want my parents or friends to know of it. For this same reason, I had never told him my last name or place of residence. At this meeting, I informed him that he must either give up all further connection with the movement he had instituted toward the regeneration of mankind, or bid me good-bye forever. He chose the latter course, although I know that his heart was fairly bursting with grief when I left him.

"'Now, that it is too late, I can fully appreciate what a grand, noble fellow he was. I offered him a million dollars to forsake the cause he had pledged himself to uphold. Think of it, one million dollars! A sum of money for which most civilized men would gladly sell their eternal souls. But John Convert, a believer in Natural Law, could not be bought at any price, and even though I offered him my hand in marriage, an offering which many Crown Princes of Europe have repeatedly begged for, still he would not recede from the grand purpose he had undertaken.

"'Well, we parted, and the next morning I boarded a steamer bound for Europe. But I was wretched and unhappy, and felt that life was a burden to me. I was unable to drive the image of John Convert out of my mind, and as I stood upon the deck of the steamer, as it passed along the river leading to the ocean. I looked back toward New York, and fancied I could see poor John standing alone, and forlorn, upon one of the docks, with his arms outstretched, sadly imploring me to return, and with a feeling of remorse I started for my stateroom to lie down and have a good cry.

"'As I hurried along the dark passageway leading to my room, I was almost startled out of my senses by coming face to face with the very man I thought I had left behind, John Convert. He appeared to be even more startled than myself, and, stepping backward a few paces, he fairly trembled, as he hoarsely exclaimed: 'My God, Arletta, is that really you?' At these words I became frightened, and as the faint rays of light from a distant port-hole fell squarely upon his face, I observed a wild, peculiar stare in his eyes, and noticed that his whole countenance was overcast by a most villainous expression. At that moment, I remembered the doctor's warning words, that he might change personalities at any time that he was subjected to severe mental excitement, and I now recognized in the man standing before me the same character I had met in Paris. Just as quickly as love had taken possession of my feelings for John Convert in the hospital, just that suddenly did it depart when I saw this detestable looking creature in front of me. In an instant he became loathsome to my sight, and without waiting for another word I rushed into my state-room and bolted the door.

"'Not once did I leave my room during that trip across the ocean, but when the steamer arrived at Liverpool, and I started to go ashore, the very first person my eyes rested upon was John Convert; and from that time on he incessantly dogged my footsteps all over Europe. The more I saw of him, the more debased and despicable he appeared to me. The good, kind, old face, that I had loved so well, had now apparently become distorted by a murderous expression, and the soulful eyes which had intoxicated me with ecstasy, now depicted the nature of a degenerate. I shunned him as I would a leper, and many times I wished that I had left him to die in the hospital, instead of aiding him to recover. He became so objectionable to my sight that I threatened to have him arrested if he did not stop following me about. But this had no effect upon him whatever, and after three long, weary months of travel on the continent, in which I attempted to elude him, without success, I finally returned to England and boarded a steamer at Southampton for New York. I fully expected to see John Convert make the voyage also, but to my surprise and great joy I saw him standing on the pier after the steamer had left her moorings and was steaming away. He stood waving his hand at me, and I watched him until beyond the range of vision, then went down to my state-room, with a feeling of relief, as though a great load had been lifted from my shoulders. One of the first things that attracted my attention after entering the state-room, was a large, well-filled envelope, lying upon the bed, and addressed to me. Tearing it open, I found an assortment of various documents, among which was the following letter.'"

"'My dear Arletta: At last realizing that you are beyond my reach and that further efforts to win your love would be useless, and feeling that after all, my affinity is not really you but she whom I recently killed, and as my conscience is torturing me until I can find no rest or contentment in life, I have decided to avenge the many crimes I have committed during the past by taking my own life, and ere you read these lines I shall be dead.

"'My life has been a most miserable failure, and were it not for the fact that during my last hours I feel a strong desire to try and make amends, through you, to the man I have been impersonating for many years, I should, quietly pass out of existence without further ado.

"'In the first place my name is not John, but Edward Convert, son of Henry Convert, and grandson of Peter Convert, who many years ago was a wealthy banker of London, England.

"'My grandfather had two sons; James, the elder, being my uncle, and Henry the younger, my father.

"'About the time my father reached maturity, both he and my uncle fell in love with beautiful twin sisters of a poor family, and in due course of time each took one as a wife. This was done in direct opposition to my grandfather's commands, and so incensed did he become over the affair, that when he died shortly afterward, it was found that he had cut them both off with a mere pittance, while the bulk of his estate which was valued at several million pounds, was to be held in trust until the eldest son of my uncle James had reached maturity, after which it was to be delivered to him intact.

"'At that time neither my father nor uncle had children, and being of different temperaments-my uncle a pious clergyman, and my father a broker with gambling tendencies-they soon parted and lost track of each other.

"'My parents emigrated to Canada and resided in Toronto for some years, in which city I was born. When I was about five years of age my mother died, and a short time later my father moved to Buffalo, N. Y., and entered into the brokerage business there. As I grew up, I was educated with the sole idea that the only purpose for which I had been created was to get money. At home I was taught by my father, in school through books, and at church by the pastor, that my success in life would be judged according to the amount of money I could accumulate. Was it any wonder, then, that I grew up to worship money as the real god, and to finally sell my soul for it? Oh, the terrible curse of money! And what an awful crime for parents to teach their children to love it! Had I not been taught from infancy to crave money, I might have become a useful member of the human family, and utilized my brain power for some worthy cause, instead of using it to scheme, cheat, steal, and even murder, in order that I might obtain it.

"Well, one day when I was about sixteen years old, my father, having just returned from one of his western trips, informed me that he had accidentally run across his brother James, the clergyman, in a little Kansas town named Eden. He said that my uncle told him that his wife had died sixteen years before, while giving birth to an only son, as they were crossing the Atlantic Ocean. Subsequently this son, who had been named John, ran away from home when he was but eleven years old, and had never been seen or heard of since. My father said that Uncle James had evidently brooded over the matter so long that he was broken down in health and could not live much longer. Then he showed me a picture of John Convert, when he was ten years old, and said that it looked exactly like me at that age. Finally, he told me that Cousin John was the sole heir to his grandfather's estate, and intimated that it would be a splendid stroke of business for me to go to Eden and pretend to be the long-lost son, and, after reaching the age of twenty-one, claim the estate as my own. My father told me that as soon as he heard my uncle's story, his well-trained financial brain had immediately formulated this excellent plan, and consequently he led my uncle to believe that he had no children of his own. He also ascertained the names of the different places where my uncle had lived during the past, and proposed that I should visit these localities and become acquainted with John's old playmates, in order to acquire a thorough knowledge of his youthful characteristics and any other useful information necessary to carry out the deception successfully.

"'Well, I entered into the plot with enthusiasm, and within six months presented myself to Uncle James as his son.

"'At first the scheme worked to perfection, and there was great rejoicing in the little town of Eden, where the Rev. James Convert was an honored and respected citizen of the community. But as time went by, my uncle apparently began to doubt my identity, for at times he would look at me long and searchingly, and then, with a sorrowful shake of the head, would remark that I lacked the character of the boy he had known as his son. So, fearing that he might ultimately discover the fraud and foil our plans, my father and I jointly murdered him by a slow process of poison. Then, with the necessary papers in my possession, and plenty of reputable witnesses from Eden to swear that I was the acknowledged son of the Rev. James Convert, at the age of twenty-one I took possession of my grandfather's vast estate in England.

"'But the fear of the rightful heir turning up sooner or later to expose the fraud began to haunt me, and, feeling my insecurity as long as he was alive, I began a long and tedious search for John Convert, which extended to all parts of the world, and covered a period of over twenty- three years, with the sole purpose of killing him if found.

"'In the meantime, fearing that my father might become conscience-stricken sooner or later, and make a confession of our crime to the authorities, I killed him also; and of the three murders, of which I am now responsible, I feel less concern over my father's death than of the other two; for was it not from him that I inherited the instincts to lie, cheat, steal, and murder for money, and by his instructions that these instincts were developed, instead of being discouraged from infancy?

"'Well, although I searched in nearly every nook and corner of the globe, I was unable to find even a clue to my missing cousin, but during that time a most peculiar affair happened, which resulted in my killing a third victim.

"'As you will remember, I met and became infatuated with you in Paris over three years ago, and then followed you to Chicago. After learning that you had secretly departed for Europe again in order to avoid me, I made up my mind to bother you no further, and taking a trip in the opposite direction I spent considerable time touring Australia, Africa and Asia. It was about two years after, while stopping at a fashionable hotel in Berlin that I discovered a young woman boarding there by the name of Arletta Fogg. So closely did she resemble you that I supposed it was you living there under an assumed name. At first when I accused her of being Arletta Wright, of Chicago, she denied it emphatically. But later, after learning that I was a millionaire, she pretended that I was right in my supposition and led me to believe that she had left home for an indefinite period owing to some family disagreement and was now traveling incognito. She permitted me to show her many attentions and gradually we became very good friends. So infatuated with her charms did I become that I was her abject slave. We went to Italy and Egypt together and I lavished money upon her without stint. I proposed honorable marriage to her a hundred times, but she always refused, saying that she preferred a free and independent life. We went to New York, and there I discovered that there were other men besides myself interested in her, and that she had two different places of residence. Several times I saw her in fashionable restaurants dining with other men, and following her one night into the Seraglio Apartments, I found that she occupied a suite of rooms there, of which I had known nothing. She was somewhat under the influence of liquor that night, and the information I secured from her was of such a kind that it almost drove me mad with jealousy, and in a fit of frenzy I stabbed her to death with her own toy dagger and left her lying on the bed. The next morning I quietly boarded the steamer for Europe, and keeping out of sight until away from land, I started to go to the purser's office to pay for my passage, when the very first person I met was you. You can well imagine how it startled me to see one whom I thought was dead. But after the first shock had passed away, and learning from the list that Arletta Wright was a passenger, I gave the whole matter thoughtful consideration and finally concluded that Arletta Fogg and Arletta Wright were two different persons and that the other was merely a beautiful adventuress and your double.

"'Well, you know the rest. You never would care for me, and as the great wealth I so wrongfully acquired cannot buy happiness of peace of mind, I shall ask God to forgive my sins and then blow out the brains that have become so useless.

"'Somewhere in this world the right John Convert may be earning his bread by the sweat of his brow, entirely ignorant of the fact that he is a millionaire by birth, for it was his father's intention never to disclose this secret to him, preferring that he should spend his time as a useful laborer, rather than a moneyed loafer, living without work. Whether he resembles me at this age or not, I cannot say. Perhaps not, for my hair has become prematurely white from sin and worry. Then again, he may wear a beard, while my face is clean shaven. But no matter where he is, what he does, or how he looks, I shall trust in you to do all within your power to try and locate him, and deliver into his hands the enclosed papers, which will be the means of restoring his possessions to him.

"'If you are fortunate enough to find him, beg his forgiveness for me, and say that the cause of all my wickedness was money, and a father who taught me to love it. With a prayer to God for mercy, I shall expect to go to heaven in spite of my sins, as I have faith in Jesus Christ, and, hoping to meet you there, I bid you good-bye until then.

"'Sincerely yours,

"'EDWARD (JOHN) CONVERT.'"

"'Notwithstanding the dreadful contents of this letter, I felt like crying with joy after reading it, as my mind once more became occupied with thoughts of the splendid character whom I had so ardently loved, but shamefully deserted in New York three months previously. I made up my mind to return and ask his forgiveness, and then join him in his praiseworthy labors of uplifting mankind. Oh! what happiness I experienced during the next few days in anticipation of seeing him again and hearing his manly voice. But alas, how little we know what sorrows are in store for us! The steamer arrived at her wharf at ten o'clock this morning, and a few minutes later. I was seated in a carriage speeding along in the direction of the Waldoria Hotel. At forty minutes past ten I inquired of the clerk for John Convert. Then came the appalling information that he was to be electrocuted at noon for the murder of Arletta Fogg. The rest seems like an awful nightmare. Getting a schedule of trains for Sing Sing, I rushed outside the hotel, and, jumping in the first cab I saw, handed the driver a roll of bills, and told him they were all his if he could get me to the depot in time to catch the eleven o'clock train. Through the streets like mad we whirled, and, reaching the station, I quickly alighted and ran to the ticket office, and from there to the train, which I boarded just as it started away. It was an express, which made no stops before reaching Sing Sing, and was due there at exactly twelve o'clock, the time set for the electrocution. I told the conductor that I would give him a million dollars if he would land me in Sing Sing fifteen minutes ahead of time, but he apparently thought I was insane, and paid no attention to my frantic entreaties to go faster. To make matters worse, the train arrived five minutes late, but, hoping against hopes, I got into a carriage and was driven to the prison.

"Here the attendants thought I was crazy, as I rushed into the reception room, crying out to stop the electrocution, and they would not permit me to see the Warden, who was in his private office. Hearing my cries, however, the Warden came out to see what was the trouble, and as quickly as possible I explained to him the circumstances surrounding the murder of Arletta Fogg, and showed him the written confession of Edward Convert. He read just enough to make sure he was right, and then with an exclamation of horror he rushed out of the office, followed by me. Through grated doors, long, dismal corridors, and a court-yard, we ran, and coming to a little, red brick house, he broke open the frame door with a crash, and hurried inside, only to find that we were just a minute too late.'"

"After a fit of sobbing, Arletta Wright quieted herself long enough to say: 'Telegraph the news to all parts of the civilized world that the State of New York has just murdered the noblest mortal of which history has ever made mention. Tell the inhabitants that through his teachings a new dispensation has sprung into existence, and that Sagemanism is born again. Publicly announce my firm belief in the beautiful principles of Natural Law, and say that henceforth I renounce all further allegiance to a religion which permits the strong to victimize the weak, and upholds a corrupt and unnatural system, which allows schemers, thieves, gamblers, sneaks, loafers, spongers, and all other kinds of human parasites to grow fat off the labors of those who toil. Say that I shall take up the work where John Convert left off, and devote the remainder of my life and all of my wealth towards the cause he advocated.'"

(THE END.)